# A Gun For Braggs' Woman

# A Gun for Braggs' Woman

## STEVE FRAZEE

**Sagebrush**
**Large Print Westerns**

**Library of Congress Cataloging-in-Publication Data**

Frazee, Steve.
A gun for Braggs' woman / Steve Frazee.
   p.    cm.
ISBN 1-57490-462-0 (lg. print : hardcover )

The CIP data was not available at the time of publication.

Cataloging in Publication Data is available from
the British Library and the National Library of Australia.

L.T.E.
Frazee

**Sagebrush Large Print Westerns** are published in the United
States and Canada by Thomas T. Beeler, Publisher, PO Box 659,
Hampton Falls, New Hampshire 03844-0659. ISBN 1-57490-462-0

Published in the United Kingdom, Eire, and the Republic of
South Africa by Isis Publishing Ltd, 7 Centremead, Osney
Mead, Oxford OX2 0ES England. ISBN 0-7531-6909-6

Published in Australia and New Zealand by Bolinda Publishing
Pty Ltd, 17 Mohr Street, Tullamarine, Victoria, Australia, 3043
ISBN 1-74030-916-2

Manufactured by Sheridan Books in Chelsea, Michigan.

# CHAPTER 1

*"You're darned right I remember her! She was about twenty-six then, I'd say. I sort of suspected that she was flat broke, but even so, she didn't have to get off at Cimarron just because her ticket said so. After all, I was the conductor, and a pretty lively young fellow in those days. You know what I mean?"* Samuel T. Franklin, retired conductor, Third Division, Denver & Rio Grande Railroad, Los Angeles, California, 1932.

DECEMBER 23, 1886. SMOKE FROM THE STOVEPIPES of the buildings jammed in the narrow valley with its ice-covered river was hanging low in the bitter air. The rails of the narrow gauge were twin bands of shiny coldness running east toward the Black Canyon of the Gunnison River and west toward Cerro Summit. The wagon road was a brown streak of frozen ruts wandering through crusted remnants of old snow.

The westbound train whistled from upriver.

Jug Ears Harris, the bigmouthed horse trader, stamped his feet on the station platform and turned up the collar of his stained sheepskin coat. "She's late again."

"What's the difference?" Pinky Bragg said irritably. "You ain't going nowhere, anyhow." He looked up Cerro Hill. He was leaving pretty soon, though not by train. In fact, he had tarried too long already.

No great shakes for looks was Pinky Bragg. His eyes were small and squinty. He didn't have much of a nose, and his mouth was a thin little gap that twisted when he

1

talked. His youthful beard was a week old, but it was only a pinkish smudge on his upper lip and on his chin. He did, however, have a snakeskin band on his black hat and a fine pair of boots with green diamonds stitched in the uppers.

"I'll take forty apiece, Jug Ears," he said. "How can you beat that?"

"By not buying at all." Jug Ears swiped his mitten across his runny nose and glanced up Cerro Hill.

"There's nobody coming!"

"Just looking, Bragg, just looking." Jug Ears grinned. When the train came in sight, he watched it with keen attention. "Most likely they had to stop to roll rocks off the tracks in the canyon, wouldn't you say?"

"You want them two horses for nothing, don't you?"

"I ain't said I wanted them at all."

"Thirty-five, and that's it."

Jug Ears peered at the oncoming engine. "From the way he whistled, I'd say it was Jake Arbaugh at the throttle."

"To hell with the train and you, too!" Pinky stomped off toward the end of the platform that overhung the creek. He looked at the road west. No one was in sight. When you took them out of a high pasture, especially in weather like this, maybe no one would miss them for a long time, but a man couldn't depend on that.

He'd brought them through town late the night before. As far as he knew, nobody had seen him. They were hid out now in the trees above Jug Ears' camp. Everything had worked out fine, except that Jug Ears, the dirty thief, had gotten cute about the whole business. He was hoping to get those two horses for about twenty-five dollars a head, that's what.

The train was grinding in, bell clanging, brakes

2

squealing. Acrid coal smoke mingled with the biting air. Fine cinders rained down on Pinky's head and shoulders, and he didn't get the collar of his sheepskin turned up before a hot one went down his neck. He cursed the cinder, Jug Ears, and the engineer all in the same breath. A dozen men had gathered now on the platform, coming from the Black Canyon Hotel, the section house, and Joe Harbor's general mercantile.

Faces behind the frosted coach windows were only pale blurs as the passengers began to stir. A porter placed a step stool on the ground. "Yes, sir, twenty minutes for lunch," he told a black-garbed man who looked like a preacher and who was hesitating on the coach platform as if doubtful about trusting his life among the loafers blocking his way to the door of the eating house.

Pinky watched the conductor helping passengers alight from the second coach. That young Sammy Franklin sort of fancied himself, what with his blue uniform and brass buttons and all. All he had to do, Pinky thought sourly, was ride back and forth on a nice warm train, telling lies to the women.

Pinky walked back to Jug Ears, who seemed to be looking for someone among the passengers. "I've decided to take thirty. Either one of them is worth a hundred, and you know it."

"Either one of them is worth a good risk for a rope around somebody's neck, and you know that, too." Jug Ears didn't even look at Pinky.

"You're trying to rob me, damn you!"

"Don't cuss me, Bragg. Man alive, look at that! Did you ever see the likes of that this side of Denver?"

For a moment Pinky didn't catch on, and then he saw the woman Jug Ears was talking about. Franklin was

3

helping her down from the second coach, smiling and nodding like some fat-assed politician.

At first glance she looked like a big woman. Her honey-blond hair was swept high on her head, and she stood real straight coming down the steps. She was wearing a fur cape that glistened with a silvery look. Once she was on the ground beside Franklin, Pinky saw that she was about as tall as the conductor, who was not a large man. She turned her head slowly, studying the town.

"You ain't going to find nothing like that short of one of them high-class fancy houses in St. Looie," Jug Ears said.

"A minute ago you said Denver. How do you—"

"I just upped my estimate by a few hundred miles, Bragg."

"You're just guessing about her."

"Hah! Look at them clothes. Look at how she's sizing things up. Do you see any other woman dressed like her?"

Pinky certainly did not. Most of the other women passengers were bundled up in plain clothes. He saw the conductor pull a carpetbag from the coach platform. The woman took it. Then Franklin hauled down a bulky canvas-wrapped bundle. "Is she getting off here?" Pinky asked.

"Looks like it."

"What for, I wonder."

Jug Ears never liked to be without an answer. "Kin," he said sagely. "She's got kin here."

"Who?"

Jug Ears gestured with his mittened hands. "Why, at one of the ranches somewhere. She's sure as hell too high-toned to be stopping here for business reasons."

4

The other loafers pushed back against Pinky and Jug Ears to make way for the passengers to reach the door of the eating room. Two of the women paused at the top of the steps to say something to each other and to glare at the blonde.

One man in a long beaver coat did not go into the steamy eating room. He lit a cigar and began to pace the platform.

Carrying the woman's luggage under one arm, Conductor Franklin piloted her up the steps with his free hand on her elbow. Oh, he was a young dandy, you bet, Pinky thought—him and his airs and them brass buttons and a white shirt. He pictured himself holding a beautiful woman's arm, talking free and easy to her. The thought sort of scared him.

She was wearing a blue velvet dress. Pinky didn't know when, if ever, he had seen a woman get off the narrow gauge in a velvet dress. As she took the last step, her long skirt lifted and Pinky saw her high-laced cloth-top shoes. They had little dabs of fur around them.

"You've been very kind, Mr. Franklin," she said.

"This is my regular run, you know, Casey. I'll be back."

Silently Pinky mimicked the conductor. *My regular run, you know* . . . Casey? What kind of name was that for a woman?

She was well aware of the hard stares of the men on the platform. She took in all the faces with a sweeping glance, but Pinky was sure she looked at him just a little longer than at any of the others.

Her eyes were dark blue in a face strong and clean, with firm cheeks bright from the cold. Pinky saw no harsh lines, no sign of hardness, nothing in her clear young features to indicate that she was what Jug Ears

5

had said. Gosh, she was pretty!

Pinky was still gaping as little Billy Masterson, the clerk at Harbor's mercantile, jumped to open the door. The woman smiled and gave him a nod of thanks, and then she was gone and Pinky was still standing with his mouth hanging, wishing he had thought to hold the door.

"No, sir," Jug Ears said, "nothing like her this side of St. Looie."

"Why not say Paris, France, being the world traveler that you are?" Tim Riley said, grinning. He was an engineer of one of the helper crews stationed at Cimarron.

"I ain't always been a horse trader, Riley. Before I lost my fortune in houses and lots—"

"Ah, I know," Riley said, "whorehouses and lots of whiskey. Now to get back to the question at hand—"

"She didn't look like no sporting-house woman to me," Pinky blurted.

"Now there's a fine innocent who should get out of the woods more often," Riley said.

Let them laugh, Pinky thought. He remembered to take a quick look up Cerro Hill before he went close to the window to peer inside. The glass was moist on the interior, so about all he could tell was that she was sitting at the counter with Franklin, while Ma Jensen took their order.

To hell with that lying Jug Ears and the rest of them, too! They didn't know everything. She was no fancy woman, no matter what the loudmouths said. Pinky tried not to hear what they were saying. He moved his head from side to side, trying to get a clear view through the window. That one look she'd given him had done something to his insides. It was sort of like when Pa and all of them had the fiddle and the harps and the banjo going. Something happened to a man then, and he forgot a lot of the mean things around him.

The pusher engine was coming off the siding to couple onto the train. Pinky wished it would make even more noise so the bigmouths talking about the woman would shut up. Shivering inside his heavy overcoat, the porter hurried up the platform steps. "Ain't you going to eat?" he asked the tall man in the beaver coat. "We only got twenty minutes."

"No, thanks. I've seen enough of your railroad sandwiches. The last ones I ordered were varnished so they could dust them off easier each time they set them out."

That brought a laugh from Jug Ears and Riley. "Say, mister," Jug Ears called, "where'd she get on at?"

The man didn't even ask whom he meant. "Denver." He laughed shortly.

Pinky glared at him. Most likely the man had tried to get gay with her and she had set him down in a hurry. When Pinky turned back to the window, he saw a large peephole where someone inside had rubbed the film away. As he bent to look through it, a boy inside pressed his face against the glass. Pinky recoiled, startled by the flat-nosed, goggle-eyed vision only a fraction of an inch away. He fell back so quickly that his foot slipped on the ice-lumpy planks and he staggered.

The loafers thought that was very funny. "What's the matter, Bragg?" Riley yelled. "Did she bite you through the glass?"

"Go to hell!" Pinky snarled. He went down the steps and walked up the tracks, intending to keep right on going, but at the corner of the section house he stopped. He could see the road on Cerro Hill quite well from where he stood. Though no one was coming, he knew it was risky to keep on hanging around town.

If she had kinfolks, why hadn't they come to meet her? He pictured himself offering to drive her to where she wanted to go. *Miss Casey, I've got a buggy over at the livery. It would be my pleasure to drive you anyplace you want to go.* And then she would smile at him and say he was very kind, and he would take her arm, and they would walk out together, and he would give the loafers a hard look to make them keep their dirty mouths shut.

Hunched against the cold, Pinky was still waiting at the section house when the train whistled and the passengers began to hurry aboard. Sure enough, Miss Casey was not among them. Pinky had thought maybe she had made a mistake and would get back on the train. Conductor Franklin was one of the last ones out of the eating house. He ought to be fired for not giving his work better attention, Pinky thought.

As soon as the passengers were out of the eating-house, the loafers all went in. Ma Jensen had them pretty well trained not to crowd her place at train time. The little engines and the coaches rocked away toward the long grind of Cerro Hill. Now the drab town seemed lifeless in the claws of winter. Pinky wanted to go back to Ma Jensen's and walk right in. Miss Casey probably would notice him again, the way she had before. But all those loudmouths in there . . .

Feeling frustrated and disgusted and all astir with the turmoil and uncertainty of youth, he went to get his horse.

Jeff Minnick, the liveryman, took Pinky's dollar and kept looking at it as he flipped it. "That big blonde in the blue dress didn't get back on the train, did she?"

Minnick didn't miss much. Him with a family, too,

the old bastard, Pinky thought. "Didn't she?"

"You was over there. What's she doing in Cimarron?"

"How would I know?"

"I just wondered." Minnick shrugged. All the Braggs, except Boston, maybe, had evil tempers. Minnick got along with them all right, though. One thing, they paid their bills without argument, which was more than he could say of some people. "Tell your pa and the boys hello for me, Pinky. I suppose you're taking home presents for them."

Pinky slapped the saddle blanket on his bay horse. "What for?"

"Christmas! Day after tomorrow is Christmas."

Pinky grunted. "The hell you say." Christmas, huh? When Ma and the girls were home, they always made a fuss about Thanksgiving and Christmas, but Pa—the only holidays he put much stock in were voting time and the Fourth of July. Still, it wouldn't be a bad idea to take some presents back to the Mesa—only Pinky had just spent his last dollar. He could get credit at Harbor's, but Pa would skin him alive if he did. Pa just didn't hold with owing nobody for nothing.

The bay horse acted up some when it hit the cold. Pinky handled it without really paying much attention. He rode up the creek to Jug Ears' camp, an old Army tent and a rope corral in the cottonwoods where a dozen shaggy horses with icicles on their jaws were waiting for Hezekiah Freeland, Jug Ears' helper, to give them their daily bait of hay.

Old Zeke—he was about forty—was frying side meat on the sheet-iron stove in the tent. He was a stringy man with a grizzled beard and an undershot jaw and a nose askew from contesting saloon bouncers. One whiff and

9

Pinky knew that he had been mixing his drinking and his cooking.

"Headed home?" he asked.

"Yeah. Soon's I talk to Jug Ears again."

"He'll be along." Zeke pulled the frying pan to the edge of the stove and lifted a jug of Forty Rod. "He never eats nowhere but in camp, unless somebody buys him a meal, and your damn town don't look like a place where anybody ever buys anything, if you ask me." He shook the jug. "Let's have one before we eat."

Whiskey and Pinky didn't get along together, but he guessed one wouldn't hurt him, considering the way things had been going. He sort of tongued the mouth of the jug so he wouldn't get too much, but old Zeke banged him on the back and said, "Take a man's pull, damn it!" Pinky got a little more than he'd figured on.

It always hit him behind the eyes first, and then it made his tongue woolly. This time was no exception, but even so, he felt pretty good after he began to eat Zeke's side meat and warmed-over biscuits. Except for a cold air run about knee-high, the tent was hotter than blazes.

"Did Jug Ears' buyer come in on the train?" Zeke speared a strip of side meat with his clasp knife and dropped it, grease-dripping hot, into his mouth.

"I didn't see none."

"We'll drink on that."

This time Pinky kept from getting a big slug, but he got enough. He could tell that it was hitting him pretty hard, but he didn't care. What he should have done, he decided, was stomp right into Ma Jensen's eating house, paying no attention to the smart alecks, and ask her if he could help her get wherever she was going.

It was not too late yet. He might have to take less

10

money than he'd figured from Jug Ears for the horses, but he'd still have plenty to hire a rig from Minnick. *Why, that's very nice of you, Mr. Bragg. I'll take your kind offer.*

Then he would help her into the buggy and fuss around her with one of Minnick's fancy lap robes, and they would go riding away together, talking gaily about a lot of things.

It was a pleasant dream, but Pinky knew it was not going to come about.

# CHAPTER 2

*"You never saw a face of such utter purity. She was in her late twenties then, I'd say. I was dealing in land and cattle on a rather large scale, buying a few hundred head of horses occasionally, so I offered her a job as bookkeeper in my Cimarron office. Fifty dollars a month. That was a lot of money in those days."* G. T. Harris, president of Blue Vista Oil Co., San Antonio, Texas.

JUG EARS HARRIS CAME IN AN HOUR AFTER PINKY HAD eaten. Zeke was telling about the men he had licked, and some he intended to lick, while Pinky, half listening, was thinking about Miss Casey. Jug Ears flung his sheepskin toward a pile of harness in one corner of the tent and said, "How much of that panther piss have you got left, Zeke?"

"This and one more jug, and by night there won't be any."

"Good. Finish it off and get the whole thing out of your system. I just got a wire that the buyer I expected

11

today will be in on the train tomorrow, so we'll be moving."

"High time," Zeke said, and took a drink.

"You won't have no trouble then getting rid of my two horses," Pinky said.

Jug Ears found a tin plate and scowled at it. "Damnation, Zeke, do you ever wash these bastardly things?"

"Not over a week ago. You getting high-toned?"

Jug Ears swiped the plate around his elbow a few times and helped himself to food. "Wasn't there no chops left on that hog?"

"We et 'em." Zeke belched.

"About those two horses—" Pinky began.

"You should have seen 'em buzzing around her in Ma's place," Jug Ears said. He crammed a biscuit into his mouth and wiped his nose with his sleeve. "Riley offered her his room and ten dollars. She just laughed at him. Howie Peters said she could stay at his place until his old lady came home. I guess you could say she got about every offer a man could think of, but she didn't bite."

"She didn't get mad?" Pinky asked.

"Mad? Hell's fire, son, what for?" Jug Ears laughed, and biscuit crumbs spewed from his mouth. "She had some pretty good propositions for a Godforsaken siding like this. Zeke, what do you make biscuits out of—pannier leather?"

"Yup," Zeke said.

"You're lying about her!" Pinky blurted.

"Don't say that, boy. Don't ever say I'm lying about anything, not in that tone of voice."

Jug Ears was a wicked fighter when he got roused, Pinky knew, but he wasn't going to back all the way down just the same. "What I mean is it just ain't so about her. That's what I mean."

"That's better, son, even if you still don't know what you're talking about. Why didn't you go in and talk to her, since you're so set on her being an angel?" Jug Ears stuffed side meat into his mouth.

He was a filthy-minded, dirty thief, that's what he was. Pinky hated the sight of him, but he had to deal with him, so he couldn't make him too mad. Besides, Pinky wanted to know more of what had happened in the eating house.

"Ma finally run us out," Jug Ears said. "Called us no better than a pack of excited dogs." He laughed.

That's just what they were, Pinky thought, but the first rotting creep of doubt entered his mind. Miss Casey should have gotten mad, real mad. Why hadn't she? "Who's her kinfolks around here? Did she say?"

"Agh! Kinfolks, my foot! She didn't know a soul in these parts. She's running plumb loose, son, just waiting to make some kind of killing."

Zeke tilted the jug. He licked his lips and spat. "She sure come to one freezing hellhole of a place to do it, is all I got to say."

"That's a fact," Jug Ears allowed. "That's what stumps me—a woman like her stopping here. I'll find out, though, before the night's over."

Pinky's food was a sour lump in his stomach. He wanted to hit Jug Ears as hard as he could. Since that was scarcely the peak of wisdom, he began to shift his hatred from the horse trader to Miss Casey herself. Jug Ears must be right. Here she'd gone and made Pinky think she was something nice and special, and all the time she was nothing but a damn old whore. All that smiling, her clothes, her highfalutin air . . . Why, she

13

was worse than some slab-jawed old blister who didn't pretend to be nothing else.

She'd made Pinky look and act silly before a bunch of men. He felt betrayed.

"She said she was looking for work." Jug Ears grinned. "So I told her she could come along with me as my cook any old time. I said I'd dump Zeke here in the crick in a holy minute if she wanted the job with me."

Pinky stared disgustedly at Jug Ears. "What did she say to that?"

"She asked what the pay was. I said twenty and a good warm place to sleep. She laughed and said that was not quite enough for her style of cooking. Oh, she's a corker." Jug Ears sucked grease off his mustache. "I still can't figure why she got off here."

In a way it was comforting to realize that there was at least one thing in all the world that Jug Ears didn't know, but Pinky didn't dwell long on the thought. There was a bitterness in him now that verged on hatred. To think that a fly-up-the-crick like her could fool everybody into thinking she was a decent woman on her way to visit kin!

Zeke finished his jug and threw it under the tent fly. It clinked as it rolled downhill on the brittle ground, and the sound made Pinky think of the cold ride home. "About them horses now—"

"Fifteen dollars."

"That's stealing!"

"Who's talking, Bragg?"

"They ain't branded."

"The gray ain't. I'll take him. You can sell the other one for wolf bait if you find a sucker."

"My gosh, Jug Ears . . . fifteen lousy dollars!"

The horse trader sucked his teeth and watched Zeke

digging into a pile of gear for his last jug. "I sure don't need no calendar when he's around. Every three months, right on the dot, he goes on a bender. I'll tell you what, Bragg, I'll throw in that rig you saw under the tree outside."

"What do I want with a pile of junk like that?"

Jug Ears shrugged. "I don't know."

"Both horses? Twenty-five bucks altogether?"

"Just the gray for fifteen. And the rig."

It was robbery, but Pinky knew it was the best he could get from Jug Ears. "Give me the money."

"The deal includes you taking a bait of hay up to the gray on your way out."

"Take it yourself," Pinky growled.

"I got to go back to town right away."

"All right, all right! Give me the money."

Jug Ears unfolded a long leather purse and took out two gold pieces. "You'll find a sack over there on Zeke's bed. The hay's under the tarp by the wagon." Funny thing, Jug Ears thought, once the Braggs made a deal, you could trust them to carry it out. He wouldn't have to go up the creek to make sure that both horses didn't follow Pinky home. Yes, sir, old Joel Bragg had raised his boys right.

Pinky disdained even to examine the warped, broken-down rig Jug Ears had given him as boot. He left it where it was, got the hay, and rode up to where the two horses were hidden in the trees. He was pretty well disgusted with the whole world by then, and the Forty Rod fumes in his head didn't help the feeling.

He dumped the sack of hay and stood watching the two horses tie into it. Fifteen dollars. The stinking thief! The gray was a fair-looking animal, but the sorrel was a scrubby brute for sure. He wondered why he'd bothered

15

to steal it, but of course in the dark and all . . . Pa and his brothers were going to laugh their heads off when they saw that sorrel. They were always making fun of the things he brought home when he went out on his own. And when he was forced to tell them that he'd gotten only fifteen dollars for the whole risk, they'd really bellow.

The cold wasn't helping clear up Pinky's head one darned bit. While he stood there waiting for the sorrel to get its share of Jug Ears' hay, the great idea came to him.

At first it seemed quite clear and simple. Then, as he muddled it around, it didn't look so good. "Naw!" he said out loud. But still he couldn't let go of the idea; it would sure make him look good at home if it worked out.

You didn't get nowhere unless you tried.

He rode back to Jug Ears' camp, leading the sorrel. Jug Ears was gone. Old Zeke was in drunken slumber in a twisted nest of greasy blankets, his jug beside him. Pinky watched him for a moment, and then he took the first saddle blanket he saw.

The scrubby sorrel justified his opinion of it when he had to hard snub it to a tree in order to saddle it. The miserable rig probably wouldn't even hold together. It did occur to him to try it and the sorrel out, but the chances were he wouldn't even have to ride it. In that case he'd throw the saddle away so there would be one less item for Pa and the boys to hoot about when he got home.

He went back into the tent. Zeke was still snoring. Pinky grabbed a gunnysack and threw in the pieces of side meat that Zeke hadn't cooked. He added the biscuits from the pan on the oven door. They clunked

16

into the sack like rocks. He found a long roll of rawhide lacing and dumped that in with the loot. Rawhide was handy any old time. Besides, it was handy to steal.

Then he took Zeke's jug of Forty Rod. If you looked at it right, he was doing Jug Ears a favor.

He took the sack up the road a short distance and hid it in the bushes behind a rock above the cut bank, where he could retrieve it easily from the saddle, and then he rode toward Cimarron to carry out his great idea.

Ma Jensen was a short, quick-moving woman who believed the best way to keep from taking guff, especially from men, was to dish it out when it appeared that they deserved it, and that was as soon as they came in view. A wandering husband and years of dealing with men at their worst—when they were in a hurry to eat— had sharpened her hair-trigger temper to a fine point.

She was alone in the eating room when Pinky walked in.

"Hello, Ma. By gosh, it's colder than—"

"If you came in to eat, say so. If you're here to slaver around like the rest of the brutes I just run out, beat it!"

"Well, I—I—"

"Make up your mind."

"I came to talk to Miss Casey, Ma. Over at the store they said she was still here with you."

"So she is. What do you want to talk about?"

Pinky was a little tired of the way he had been treated that day, and now a woman was jumping on him. "About a job, if it's any of your business."

"You! What kind of job, if I may be so bold as to ask?"

"It's none of your business. If she wants a job, it's her I got to talk to."

Ma shook her head unbelievingly. The squint-eyed whelp looked like he'd been drinking, but maybe it was the cold that had made his eyes so red. She jerked her hand toward the kitchen. "In there, young mister."

Pinky was taken aback to find Miss Casey washing dishes at the tin sink. She'd changed her clothes and skinned her hair back real tight on her head, like Ma's. She was wearing a big white apron, and her face was flushed from the steamy sink. He had trouble reconciling her with the woman who had gotten off the train.

"You working here now, Miss Casey?"

"For a while." She studied him quietly. "I saw you on the platform a while ago, but you didn't come inside with the others, did you?"

Pinky's heart jumped. By gosh, she really had noticed him. "Naw. I don't hang around unless I got business." He introduced himself. The woman nodded and went on working. "I got a job if you want one."

She looked at him warily. "Yes?"

"Cooking at my ranch."

"Your ranch?"

"Well, Pa's and all of us. My ma done run off and left us a couple of months back, and we've been in bad shape ever since. Pa's got a kind of touchy stomach. None of us can cook a lick, and—"

"Why did your ma leave, Mr. Bragg?"

Pinky batted his eyes. He'd figured it would make a little sympathy for his cause if Miss Casey thought they had been deserted, but for a moment he couldn't think of a good lie to keep the first lie going.

He didn't have to strain himself. Standing in the doorway, where she'd been all the time, Ma Jensen said, "His ma and his two sisters went back to Kansas for a

18

visit. Mrs. Bragg has been poorly ever since a cow kicked her in the belly."

"That's what I was trying to get at." Pinky didn't feel too steady, it was so doggone hot in the kitchen. He watched Miss Casey get a big teakettle and carry it from the stove to scald the dishes.

"How many are in your family?" she asked.

"Five men, of sorts." Ma made it sound pretty bad.

"What's the pay?" Miss Casey asked.

"Thirty dollars a month." Pinky didn't know whether that was high or low, or where it was coming from, either.

"And when does the job start?"

"What? Oh, right away." Pinky couldn't believe his ears. He'd had the idea, sure, but down deep he knew he had never really believed that she would listen. "I'm leaving right away."

"I'll say you are," Ma said. "You and your big, fat job!"

Miss Casey shook her head at Ma. "Let him talk."

"I did," Pinky said. "That's about it."

Clouds of vapor from the sink made a misty veil around Miss Casey's head for a moment. Even in the different clothes she was about as pretty a woman as Pinky ever hoped to see. He thought it was a darned shame that she had to be what she was.

"Very well, Mr. Bragg," she said. "I'll talk to Ma, and then I'll give you an answer. Say, ten minutes?"

"You—you will?" Pinky knew he should not have given away his surprise like that, but the words just slipped out.

"Pinky Bragg, does your pa know about this?" Ma demanded.

"Sure. He said when I left to see if I could find

somebody to cook for us. He's got a weak stomach and—"

"I know, I know! And if you ask me, Casey would have a weak head to believe anything you've said." Ma waved Pinky toward the eating room. "You wait out there while we settle this."

The eating room was just as hot as the kitchen. Pinky didn't feel too good, but he decided to stick it out and overhear what Ma was going to tell Miss Casey. The two women stopped that by going back into Ma's living quarters and closing the door, so Pinky went on outside to get himself a little fresh air.

He knew there wasn't much chance that Miss Casey would go with him, not after Ma Jensen got through talking to her. But just suppose she did say yes!

What a Christmas present she would be for Pa and the boys!

Pa had been on goat pasture ever since Ma left to visit her folks in Kansas, and the boys—they hadn't been to no town since they sold that last wagonload of Chamberlain's beef to the butcher shop in Lake City a month back.

What a high old time there'd be on the Mesa if he came riding in with a fancy woman! Nobody would even take a second look at the no-good sorrel. They wouldn't have time to laugh at Pinky. They'd think he was pretty doggone smart and clever.

Yes, sir, there'd be some doings at the Bragg place.

And best of all, Pinky would be revenged on that high-toned whore for her trying to make a fool out of him.

# CHAPTER 3

*"One of the so-called bad ones shot me, and a couple of what we called good ones shot at me, so I guess I know a little bit about women. It makes me laugh when I read that we had only two kinds of females in the early West. Women weren't one bit different than they are now."* Jock Jennings, Gunnison County pioneer and game warden, Gunnison, Colorado, 1928.

MA JENSEN SPOKE FORTHRIGHTLY AND WITH HEAT. "The Braggs are the worst thieves that ever came down the pike. Why, they even got rubber linings in their pants pockets so they can steal soup. They live in a shanty up on Sapinero Mesa someplace. If the men in this country had any gumption, they'd have burned that boars' nest out long ago and hung every male Bragg.

"Everybody knows they're cattle rustlers and horse thieves, but that ain't all. They'll take pigs, chickens, clotheslines, or outhouses. I hear they got a mower up there in a meadow that they stole from the U.S. Army itself. Joel, the old man, is about half smart. Come election time, he can always dig up a pile of votes for the crooks that run this county.

"Eldon, the oldest boy, looks like an ape, and he just about is. I seen him almost break a man in two with his bare hands there by the section house one time. Harve, he fancies himself as a lady-killer. Boston—well, he might have been about half civilized if he'd had the chance. You've seen what Pinky is like. So that's the Bragg tribe for you, and I don't know why you even

21

bothered to listen to that lying Pinky."

"Do they keep their agreements?" Casey was standing at a window.

"Yeah, they do," Ma said grudgingly. "Of course, the devil has been known to do that, so you can't say it's any great virtue, coming from the Braggs. But you don't have any agreement, only with Pinky, and he was lying about talking to his pa. I'll go chase him away."

"No, don't do that."

"Honest to God, Casey! You can't be serious."

Casey scrubbed a little peephole in the frosty glass. She looked beyond the town to the narrow road lifting toward the snow-patched hills. It had been a broad and easy road she had followed for three years, since that early morning when she had crept out of her father's comfortable farmhouse in Illinois to run away with Billy Carpenter, who had been full of interesting tales of traveling and of far places.

She had told Billy that she was twenty-one when she was actually sixteen.

They were married that afternoon. Two days later they were in St. Louis on their honeymoon. Casey had been quite happy, except for a nagging feeling of guilt about her parents. It was not that she regretted running away from them, but that she knew her act had hurt them. Still, she'd had to go. Her parents' thinking was of a time and world that were not for her; they just couldn't understand that life reached far beyond the acres that Great-grandfather McGillivray had settled on in the dim past.

She had to go, and so she took the jump.

For six months she persisted with the idea that marriage to Billy Carpenter was the answer to her yearning. After a week in St. Louis he had enough money left to buy a new supply of lightning rods, so they set out traveling to far places, which consisted of large sections of Iowa and Missouri. It was interesting, yes, but one day it struck Casey that she wasn't seeing anything greatly different from the country where she had grown up.

Billy hadn't lied to her or misled her. She had done that to herself. Nor did he desert her. He never would have left her. She, instead, left him when they returned that winter to St. Louis for a new supply of lightning rods.

Poor Billy. She liked him, and it wasn't easy to hurt him, to leave him standing in the hotel room with that stricken little-boy look. But she didn't love him and never had, though she had thought differently six months before. Now she knew he had been no more than a way to escape the smothering confines of a life that was stifling her. Sooner or later she would leave him, so she did it sooner, as honestly as possible. Again her regret was only for the hurt she was leaving behind, not the step she was taking.

There was a year as a domestic in a mansion on the bluffs above the muddy river. She did her work well. The Desbien family treated her well. But it was too much like being home. From there she went, with her eyes wide open, to Edith Leduc's place—a deliberate step which she never denied, not even to herself.

Miss Leduc ran a quiet, orderly establishment, a place, as she put it, for the companionship of refined young ladies. Any woman could go to bed with a man, but could she talk to him with grace and poise, carry on an intelligent conversation for an hour? Ah, young ladies, that is most important, too!

Casey was rather surprised to discover that many men

did come to Miss Leduc's place merely to talk, to drink her imported wines and brandies, to lounge in elegant surroundings, and often to leave with no further demands upon the hospitality of the establishment. While it was by no means a center devoted only to the promotion of culture, Casey did learn a great deal other than how to make a man happy in bed during the two years she was there. Miss Leduc spoke five languages fluently. She imparted to Casey conversational competence in French and Spanish, in addition to improving her English.

And Casey Leclair also learned that an intelligent conversation with a man was five percent talk on the woman's part and ninety-five percent on the man's side.

She refused six offers of marriage, four of which were splendid opportunities, according to Miss Leduc, who was proud and happy when one of her young ladies—she abhorred the word 'girls'—made a good marriage. She was fond of boasting that not one of them had ever failed in matrimony, and that several of her graduates were in very high places, all of which was quite true.

"I cannot understand you, Miss Leclair. I know you do not have the great enthusiasm for your position here, although you are doing very well, but still you refuse to marry a man like Mr. Gillaspey, a most excellent gentleman of both wealth and position. You realize that time is quite short in our profession, do you not?"

Time was driving Casey, but not in the way Miss Leduc meant. The years were getting away. Already she had made two ill-considered leaps. Another hasty marriage would merely be a third jump to nowhere. Though the details were vague, she knew she wanted some definite plan of living far different from anything

24

she had experienced so far.

"Are you serious about going up to the Braggs'?" Ma asked.

"I think so."

Ma shook her head. "You know that stammering young idiot didn't have cooking in mind. You know that, don't you?"

"I know," Casey said tonelessly.

Ma was outraged. "I made a mistake about you, young lady. I swallowed your story about wanting an honest job."

Casey turned from the window and looked directly at Ma Jensen. "I told you the truth. If I go with him, it will be only as a cook."

The older woman's stare was harsh and doubting. She understood men well enough because she operated from the premise that they were no good from the start, and then revised her opinion downward, but women were not so easily understood. She kept staring at Casey. After a time she nodded. "I've never heard anything like it in my life, but I know you're telling the truth."

"Thank you."

Ma scowled. "All right, I believe you, but what makes you think the Braggs will? Once you walk into that boars' nest, you're at their mercy, and you know what I mean."

"They're not complete savages, I hope."

"The hell they ain't! They're worse than most men, and that's about as low as you can get." Ma folded her arms. "We know that Pinky was lying faster than a dog can trot about his pa asking him to find a cook. A cook! What those renegades need most of all is a hangman. What do you think the old man is going to do when Pinky comes dragging you in like a wet kitten? Do you

25

think he'll—"

"You said the Braggs honored their agreements."

"It ain't *their* agreement. It's that snot-nosed Pinky's idea of doing something smart."

"How do I know he wasn't telling the truth?"

"Hah!" Ma waved her hands like she was fighting gnats. "The Bragg never lived that told the truth."

"If Pinky lied, then I'll have to settle the problem with the father when I meet him."

"Casey, you can't do it. I won't let you go up there."

"You've been very kind, Mrs. Jensen, and I thank you."

Ma sighed and shook her head. "You're going to do it?"

"Yes."

Once more Ma studied her intently. "I don't figure you out at all, but . . . well, it's your life."

"Exactly."

"Can you cook at all?"

"Yes."

Ma grunted. "That'll be a great surprise to them." She took some comfort from the thought that Joel Bragg would most likely drown Pinky in the spring and send Casey packing the moment he heard of the deal. "Come back and stay with me when it blows up. Jensen is off on one of his big mining deals somewhere, and I won't see hide nor hair of him until his belly starts flopping against his backbone again. You can help me around here until you work out something better."

"Thank you. I'll keep that in mind."

"No, you won't," Ma said. "I can tell you don't figure on coming back, so don't be polite. You're not hiding from some man, are you?"

"No."

26

Ma glanced at the blue velvet dress lying on the bed. "You're going horseback, you know." She waited hopefully.

"I can ride."

"And what will you wear?"

"I was wondering if you'd lend me a pair of your husband's pants. I'll see that they're returned."

"Jensen's pants! Merciful heavens! What will people say?"

Casey smiled. "Aside from you, I doubt that anyone is thinking very kindly of me, anyway."

Ma went to a dresser. "All right, young lady, since we're wearing Jensen's clothes, we'll start from the skin out." She dragged forth a pair of long red woolen drawers. She took other garments from nails in a curtained-off corner closet, throwing everything on the bed as she found it. "Put on everything you can, and then you'll likely freeze. There you are. I'll go tell that snot-nose you've made up your mind."

Entering the eating room, Ma glared when she saw that the loafers she had twice run out were now back with recruits. "If there's a dime among the lot of you, let's hear about it. Otherwise, out!" Pinky wasn't there. Ma hoped he'd lost his nerve and run away. "Well, my fine gentlemen?"

"In tribute to your gentle manner, I'll be having a cup of your wondrous coffee, fair lady," Tim Riley said.

Everyone wanted coffee. Ma served them quickly.

"What's Pinky Bragg doing hanging around outside?" a man asked.

"I've no idea," Ma snapped. "I've enough scalawags in here without worrying over Pinky Bragg."

As soon as she had a chance, she put her heavy coat on and went out to him. "She'll be ready in a few minutes. Take the horses around in back. There's no need to have the whole dog pack underfoot when she leaves."

"You mean she said she's going?"

"I'm more surprised than you. Providing the advance is paid, she'll be ready in a few minutes."

"What's the advance?"

"It's plain to see you've never hired anyone before. A month's wages, if you please, and be quick about it before I catch my death of cold."

"Thirty dollars," Pinky mumbled. "I only got fifteen, and I was figuring to buy—"

"Give it to me. It's too cold to argue. I'll see if she'l' take that little, although it's against regulations." Ma held her hand out.

Pinky parted with the money, and then he asked, "What regulations? Suppose she don't stay?"

"It's far more likely she won't even go, considering such a small advance, but I'll see. Now take the horses around in back, I said, and if you let one of the brutes knock my wood stack over, I'll dent your thick head with a brakeman's club."

Ma went whisking back inside.

Pinky didn't move for a moment. She was going to do it. By gosh, Miss Casey was taking the offer. It hit him; he had done the impossible.

Excitedly he ran to get the horses.

# CHAPTER 4

*"You mean you think it's cold at thirty-five below zero? I guess you've never seen it get really cold in this country. Did you ever hear about the big flu*

28

*epidemic they had in Crested Butte years ago? A lot
of people died, and there was no way to dig graves.
They got around that by standing the bodies outside
for a few minutes and then they drove them into the
ground with pile drivers."* Steve Waters, pioneer
rancher, Saguache and Gunnison Counties,
Colorado, 1932.

A BLAST OF FRIGID AIR ROLLED ACROSS THE BACKS OF
the loafers in the eating room as Ma Jensen held the
door open to see if Pinky was going to get started or just
stand there with his mouth drooping.

"Put the board in the hole, Ma," Jug Ears complained.

"For a man that lives in a tent, you've suddenly
gotten mighty delicate," Ma said. She walked briskly
toward the kitchen, her hand fisted around the two gold
pieces Pinky had given her.

"Where's your help, Ma?" Jug Ears asked. "We
promise to behave ourselves this time."

"Indeed you will, you—" Ma relented a little. "She'll
be out in a bit. Just stay where you are and help
yourselves to more coffee." She went on into the
kitchen.

Riley looked at Jug Ears with a thoughtful
expression. "Such great and sudden kindness
overwhelms me." He closed one eye. "Tell me, what's
Bragg doing outside, and him with two horses by the
section house?"

"They're his horses, all right, and he went thumping
that way just after Ma come back in."

Riley gestured toward the back wall. "Is it possible
that young Bragg and her—Ah, no!"

"Naw!" Jug Ears agreed.

They heard Ma bang the door to her living quarters.

29

Then she moved pots around on the stove. She came into the eating room and stoked the big heater.

"I thought you said Miss Casey was coming out," Riley said.

Ma did not snap his head off with her answer. "Oh, she'll be along directly. She's resting after her trip."

Riley rolled his eyes at Jug Ears. After Ma returned to the kitchen, Riley rose and left quietly. He found Pinky behind the building with his two horses, just getting ready to try out the sorrel. "You figuring on company, Bragg?"

"None of your damn business," Pinky said from force of habit, and then he reconsidered. He was taking Miss Casey right from under the noses of all the smart alecks like Riley. It was a pretty big thing. Instead of trying to hide the fact, like Ma Jensen wanted, he deserved to brag about it. "Sure, I'm going to have company. Miss Casey is going with me."

"Going where?"

"Wherever I say. Right now we're going home."

Riley laughed. "Fat chance!"

"All right, just hang around and see for yourself. Get all your bigmouthed friends out here, too." Pinky was feeling rather pleased with himself. When he grabbed the saddle horn, he realized that the saddle had a broken tree, but even that didn't diminish his good spirits. He swung up expertly.

The sorrel hunched. It took a few trembling steps, and then it began to loosen up. It didn't buck very hard, though. Pinky headed it into the street, figuring to let it take a short, hard run, but it gave up so quickly that he changed his mind about letting it work off steam. He rode back to Riley and jumped down.

"What's so funny about her going with me, Mr.

Railroader?"

"It would be even funnier if I believed it."

Pinky grinned. "Stick around."

They didn't have to wait long. Casey came out the back door, carrying her carpetbag and the bulky package. After he recovered from his astonishment at seeing her in men's clothing, Riley trotted over to help her with the luggage. "Now what's this wild story I've been hearing about him taking you somewhere?"

"I don't know what wild story you're talking about. Mr. Riley."

"Him! He said you were going with him."

"I am."

"See!" Pinky yelled.

"What would you go with him for?"

"I have a job at his father's ranch. I'm going to cook for them."

"Ow!" Riley howled. "Ow, no! I've got to talk to you about this."

"The talking is done. It's all settled, Mr. Riley. Now if you'll be kind enough to give me the bag after I'm mounted . . . I'm sure Mr. Bragg can handle the package if you'll pass it up to him." Casey took the reins of the bay.

Pinky looked sourly at the bulky parcel. "What's that thing? I ain't toting nothing like that on a—" He stopped talking to watch the woman mount. She went up easily. Gosh, those pants she had on!

Jug Ears and the whole band of loafers came around the building in time to see Miss Casey handle the cold horse. It buck-jumped some, sidled around, and shook its head. The stirrups were a mite long for her, Jug Ears observed, but she made out all right. Fine balance and knee grip, he noted. But those pants. Hell's fire and

31

little fishes! The pants legs worked up from the gyrations of the horse, and he saw red underwear above the tops of her shoes with the fancy dabs of fur.

She rode over to Riley. "If you'll give me the bag, please."

"First I'd like the truth. He's taking you to your kinfolks, ain't he?"

"No. I told you where I'm going."

"Ah! I've got it. You're kin of the Braggs themselves, desperate as the thought is."

"I am not. The bag, please, Mr. Riley."

Riley looked around helplessly. "She's leaving us, boys, off to the wild woods, amongst the ferocious animals and beasts, and with the likes of himself there."

Pinky was not paying much attention; he was too busy staring with enormous dislike at the big parcel. Riley gave the bag to Casey, and then he put his fleece-lined gloves in her lap. "Though you've spurned my lovely advice and broken the heart of me terrible, you can't be riding on a day like this without warm gloves."

Casey gave him a quick, warm smile. "Thank you."

Now Riley hefted the package. He looked at Pinky.

"What is that thing?" Pinky asked.

"My mirror," Casey said. "It goes where I go."

"I ain't carrying no looking glass that size on no horse. We got a ways to ride, I guess you don't seem to know."

"If I go, so does the mirror, Mr. Bragg."

"Atta girl!" Jug Ears yelled. His cohorts supported him.

"I can plainly see it's impossible for the lad to handle such a thing," Riley said. "As I deduced from the very start, the whole affair is a huge mistake. Here, I'll help you down."

32

"You leave her be!" Pinky yelled. He mounted. "Give me the danged thing."

Riley shook his head. "I have grave doubts about—"

"Hand it up here!"

The onlookers licked their freezing chops in anticipation built by the innocent gleam in Riley's eyes. They nudged each other and kept their faces sober. Riley lifted the mirror for Pinky to take. The horse sidled.

"Let go of it!" Pinky squawked.

"I must make sure your grip is firm."

The rider had one hand on the mirror. He was off balance in the crooked saddle. Someone broke an icicle from the overhang of an outhouse and tossed it against the hind legs of the horse, and at the same time Riley seemed to lose his balance on a bit of ice. He staggered backward with the package, making a loud yell. Pinky barely got himself straight in the saddle as the horse bolted. It knocked over one end of Ma Jensen's neatly stacked firewood and headed for her clothesline.

"Whoa, you son-of-a-bitch!" Pinky howled, an instant before the wire took him across the chest and spun him out of the saddle. He lit in a pile of tin cans and garbage with a clattering impact that knocked the wind out of him.

And the spectators warmed themselves with laughter.

"I was afraid he couldn't handle it," Riley said. "Now, Miss Casey, we'll all go inside and—"

She was turning her horse, going after the sorrel, which paused only to kick the door off the section crew's outhouse when the trailing reins tangled in a pile of ties close by, and then the sorrel got its directions and galloped down the road toward Cerro Hill, going home. The loafers ran around the building to get a better view

33

of the race. "Go, you bangtail, go!" Jug Ears yelled, rooting for the sorrel.

"If he gets clean away, I doubt Bragg can find another horse in the whole town with which to steal Miss Casey away, eh, boys?" Riley said. "Run, you bangtail, run!"

But the bangtail was no match for Pinky's bay. Casey caught the sorrel and started back with it. "Ah, what a rider she is, to our great misfortune," Riley sighed. "Let us go back and see if Bragg has luckily broken his neck."

Pinky was all right. He had scrabbled about in the garbage pile with his mouth flopping like a hen-house door in the wind, until he got his breath back, and now he berated Riley most profanely.

"I was but doing my duty," Riley protested, "handling a delicate bit of furniture with great caution."

"You kicked the horse in the belly!" Pinky accused.

"Tch, tch! These honest witnesses will bear out the fact that I was but acting in the best interests of everyone."

Pinky expressed his opinion of the honest, grinning witnesses. He retrieved the mirror and laid it on the roof of the outhouse, where he could easily take it aboard without any of Riley's questionable help.

Casey returned with the horses. Pinky tightened the cinch on the sorrel. He mounted and got the mirror under his arm without incident, though the horse laid its ears back and rolled its eyes.

Casey and Pinky Bragg went up the road.

"I had a fine future planned for her," Riley mused sadly.

They all felt the same way.

"She don't know what's she getting into," Jug Ears mourned. "And to think she could have had a job with me!"

"Ow!" said Riley. "In that case, she's better off with the Braggs, heartrending though the thought is."

"Let's not stand here," someone said. "I'm freezing."

"Work will warm you all." Ma Jensen was standing there with a brake club in her hand. "First the woodpile, and then fix that clothesline."

Still in sight of the town, Casey realized that she was colder than she had ever been before in her life. She remembered times in western Illinois and on the Missouri River when the dampness crept through all the clothing one could put on and made the body miserable, but that had been only an inconvenience compared to the solid, windless clamp of frigidity she felt around her now. It was a sharpness in the lungs, a stiffness around the eyes, a hard, formless grip on the feet and legs.

"How far is it to your father's place, Mr. Bragg?"

Pinky had been glancing back, shifting the mirror from arm to arm. "We ain't even out of town yet." He looked at her sidewise. "We won't make it tonight, if that's what you're wondering about."

"That's exactly what I was wondering about. Where will we stop?"

Pinky grinned. "I'll find someplace. Don't worry about it."

"Neither one of us will have anything to worry about as long as we remember one thing, Mr. Bragg."

"Yeah? What's that?"

"That I'm going to your father's ranch to cook. Do you understand?"

"Sure!" Pinky's mouth twisted into a grin. "Sure, we're all going to remember that real good."

Once in an angry slip from dignity, when the young

35

scion of a wealthy merchant had tried to tear up her place, Miss Leduc had likened the overeager youth to "a young hog rooting in the manure pile for the first time." It was a description that fitted Pinky aptly, Casey thought.

She could handle him all right, she was sure, but he was only the youngest of the Braggs. Now that she had time to give her move second consideration, she granted more weight to some of the rather large flaws that Ma Jensen had dwelled upon. Though she could discount some of Ma's attitude toward the Braggs, since Ma was working hard to convince herself that she hated all men, Casey still could not totally ignore what Ma had told her.

Maybe it was the awful cold that was helping give her doubts. When Pinky twisted around again, she, too, looked back at the town.

She saw an engine chugging toward a switch. That was the only sign of life. It wasn't much of a town, but it held warmth and a woman who had befriended her. Before long the eastbound train would stop. Tomorrow there would be other trains. No matter how mean and remote the town was, it was closely linked to escape.

Or at least to change.

Where she was going . . . Where *was* she going?

Ahead, there was a turn in the road that would cut the town from view. Suddenly that turn represented irrevocable decision. Everything before had been quick action without thought, starting from the moment she had left home.

Everything, it seemed to her. Her going to Miss Leduc's house and her departure from it. Her trip to Denver on a crowded train and then her buying of a ticket as far beyond as her money would allow. None of those acts had been sharply struck decisions, but a desperate, uncertain drifting.

Maybe her acceptance of Pinky's spurious offer had been in the same pattern. But now, she told herself, it was different. If she went around that bend ahead, she would be deliberately taking a sharply angled turn in life. It would be starting again, in a slow, hard way, a careful searching for signposts that she had missed entirely before.

But the move was weighted against her in advance, for the agreement she had made was lopsided. She was the only one who intended to abide by it.

Pinky certainly did not intend to hold to the face of the contract, and it was not likely that his family would, either. Convincing them all that she intended to abide by it might be an impossible task.

She stopped her horse suddenly.

"What's the matter?" Pinky cast an anxious look at the sky.

Casey looked back at the town. It was no longer form and substance, only a symbol of her former life. It was there, and it was easy to go back. The cold alone seemed enough justification for quitting now.

"Come on," Pinky said. "We've got no time to fool around. It looks like a storm coming."

Casey studied him with clear detachment. His features were all squinched up with complaint, as if they were trying to huddle against each other in the cold. He was undoubtedly the most unpromising male she had ever had anything to do with. And she had placed herself in his hands.

No, he doesn't matter, and neither does his family, whatever they are. I'm placing myself in my own hands.

After another long moment in the still, bitter air, she

sent her horse on up to the turn of the road and went around it.

Now it was done. Now, she could tell herself that she had made a choice. But a last doubt remained. Out of the frying pan, into the fire . . .

# CHAPTER 5

*"Women often stood those hardships better than men."* Joe Cuenin, veteran U.S. Forest Ranger, Marshall Pass, Colorado, 1924.

HER FEET WERE ALREADY BECOMING A PROBLEM. Casey tried to work her toes, but her shoes were so tight that all she could do was flex her ankles. She slipped her hands out of Riley's big gloves and tightened the woolen scarf around her head. Before long she would have to do something about her feet.

Near Jug Ears' camp Pinky rode over to the cut bank and laid the mirror on a rock. He stretched down and hoisted a gunnysack from the bushes and tied it to his saddle horn. "Just some stuff I left here," he explained. He rode on.

"You left the mirror, Mr. Bragg."

"I sure did."

Casey's horse was anxious to follow the other animal. She had to hold it in hard. When Pinky realized that she wasn't coming, he stopped and looked around, keeping an eye on the tent in the cottonwoods. "I ain't taking it no farther. It's caused me enough grief already."

"Then I go no farther."

"You won't need it."

"The mirror goes with me, Mr. Bragg."

Pinky kept watching the tent. "You've got my money. Just remember that."

"You can have it back right now!"

"Don't yell." Pinky rode back to her. "You just want an excuse to go back, don't you?"

She waited.

Mumbling a curse, Pinky took the mirror from the rock. Casey knew from his expression that he intended to get rid of it as soon as possible.

They went on up, under the rapidly closing overcast. Two frozen ruts in a poor road winding through the hills. If there were mountains beyond, the approaching storm hid them. They met a wagon loaded with raw yellow lumber, driven by a bearded man with a woman's scarf around his head, under his shapeless hat. He looked at Casey only briefly, and then he gave Pinky a hostile glance, "Hi-ya, Bragg."

Then, having passed, he turned suddenly to stare at Casey and kept looking back until the wagon hit a wrenching sag in the road.

"They all look at you, don't they?" Pinky said.

"I suppose it is odd to see a woman in these clothes."

"That ain't what I mean."

Young hog, she thought. Under better circumstances she would have driven him back in confusion upon himself.

There were problems more urgent than putting this half-grown man in his place. She stopped the bay and got down, and when her feet touched ground, she would have fallen if she had not been clinging to the saddle horn.

"Now what?" Pinky grumbled.

The air bit savagely at Casey's fingers as she opened her bag and got out a mink cape old Mr. Winters had

39

given her one afternoon in front of the parlor fire, along with a lecture on the greatness of St. Louis in fur-trading days. "The matching of furs is an art in itself. These are from a small animal not generally sought, but you will note . . ."

That was in another time, another world. Standing on part of the cape, Casey ripped it in two. She tore the black silk lining out and threw it aside. The earth sent a massive coldness through her clothes as she sat there unlacing her shoes with stiffening fingers. That done, she began to bind the hides on her feet, fur side in.

Pinky deposited the mirror on a patch of snow above the road. He got down to pick up the cape lining. While he was tying it over his head and ears, the sorrel turned and tried to trot away. He caught the trailing reins just as the horse was gathering speed. "I'll kill that horse yet."

Again he started to ride on without the mirror. Awkward in her fur wrappings, Casey went across the road and picked it up and stood waiting for him to come back. He went a hundred yards before he turned to look. He hesitated, and then he came storming back and grabbed the reins of the bay.

"The deal's off! Keep the lousy money and your old looking glass, too. I'm going home." Leading the bay, Pinky rode away.

"Wait a minute," Casey called.

He came back, grinning. "Yeah, I thought so."

Casey was digging in her carpetbag. She found the two gold coins and threw them on the ground in the man's direction. She picked up the bag and the mirror and started down the hill toward Cimarron.

"Go ahead! See if I care."

Pinky watched her for a while. She wobbled some in

her clumsy footgear, but she continued to move away steadily. He picked up the money and set out after her. "You're the craziest-acting woman I ever knew. Here. Take your darned money and let's quit fooling around."

"I'm not fooling, Mr. Bragg."

Pinky had just come to the same conclusion. "What's so precious about that looking glass?"

What indeed, Casey asked herself. Billy Carpenter had given it to her when, after two years' separation, he found out where she was. He had not come to see her. He sent the gift by messenger, with no note. "Carpenter? I do not know this man. Who is he?" Miss Leduc asked.

"I think he was one of that group from New Orleans who was here last month."

"I do not recall that name, which is strange because I am not one to forget names and faces . . . But it is a fine mirror."

Yes, it was a fine mirror. Casey knew why Billy Carpenter had sent it, and that was why she put it in a closet and never looked into it. She was beginning to understand now why she had taken it with her when she left.

"What's so all-fired wonderful about that looking glass?" Pinky demanded.

The only answer Casey cared to give was, "I told you it goes where I go."

Just plain woman stubbornness, Pinky decided. Doggone her, she didn't act like a sporting-house woman.

"All right, I'll take the looking glass."

Casey didn't stop walking.

"I said I would!"

"And you'll break it or leave it behind as soon as we're so far away you think I won't be able to go back.

41

I want you to understand, Mr. Bragg, that I'll return if that happens, no matter how far we've gone."

By Ned, she was a tough customer about that glass. "All right, all right, I'll take it all the way."

"Your promise on that?"

Pinky sighed. "I promise. Here's your money. Give me the son- —the danged thing and let's stop this foolishness."

They came to a summit not long after they reversed direction, a break from which Casey saw a long, snowy valley with dark trees on the far side. Against the toe of the far hill were the brown blots of buildings. "Is that your ranch down there?"

Moisture spun from Pinky's nose as he shook his head.

Just as they went over the break and started down the hill, the whistle of the eastbound train came up to them in a thin and lonely wail like a distant crying for something lost and regretted.

And then the storm broke against them—small, hard flakes of snow that scratched at their clothes. The valley below was blotted out. Casey heard the whistle one more time.

She fastened the top button of Jensen's old jumper, remembering how hot it had been on the train. The faces she had seen there were indistinct now, except for the chubby countenance of the young news butch, who had treated her like any of the other women passengers.

"Stinking snow," Pinky grumbled. "I knew it was due."

Casey soon lost all sense of perspective and direction. In an incredibly short time the snow began to level out variations of color in the landscape. It put fresh finish on the glazed patches of old snow, covered the brown earth, and smoothed away the outlines of the road. Only the steep sides of the cut bank and the scrub oaks resisted the change.

A half hour after the onset of the storm, the flakes became bigger, softer, and then they clung to everything they touched. The cold seemed worse than ever.

Pinky's horse suddenly decided it wanted to go back. It stopped and stood quietly for a moment, and then it tried to whirl. The rider jerked its head around and forced the reluctant sorrel on down the road. Not long afterward Pinky was shifting the mirror from one side to the other when some of the cord binding loosened. A flap of canvas fell down and brushed over the neck of the horse.

The horse left the road and bolted straight downhill.

Casey saw it slide on its haunches into one gully. It lunged up the other side, with Pinky fighting to get it under control. Then horse and rider disappeared into a second gully and did not emerge.

Her own horse did not want to leave the road. It kept turning back from the drop, but she forced it down the plunge. Pinky was caught under the sorrel, which was lying on its side in a steeply pitched snowdrift at the bottom of a gully.

"Are you hurt?"

"My leg's busted. Help me!"

The crust kept giving way under Casey as she wallowed out to help him. She got hold of him under the arms and tugged.

Pinky groaned. "Take it easy! My leg's busted."

The sorrel began to struggle to get up. Because of the slant of the snowdrift, it was threatening to roll on both of them. Casey ignored the man's groans and dragged as hard as she could. Pinky came free. "My leg!" he howled. When the threshing horse rolled toward them, he scrambled on hands and knees out of the way as quickly as Casey.

Once on its feet, the sorrel started to run down the gully. Casey leaped and grabbed the reins. The frantic animal dragged her off her feet before she got it stopped.

She looked around and saw Pinky on his feet. He rubbed his leg, then raised and lowered it slowly. He took a few steps, and then he looked at Casey with a foolish expression. "I'd a-swore it was busted."

Casey began to laugh.

After a time Pinky grinned sheepishly. "I guess it was the crust popping when we hit, instead of my leg bone."

Casey found the mirror wedged in the oak brush near the first gully. She shook it gently and heard no tinkle of glass. She tried to carry it back to the road, leading her horse, but the bindings on her feet had come loose. She stumbled and tripped over the laces. In falling she caught the stirrup of the bay, and the horse dragged her and the mirror back on the road where she had dropped her carpetbag before going to aid Pinky.

Pinky took a more roundabout route. He tied his horse to a scrub oak before he began to rid himself of snow packed under his outer clothing. "I'm going to kill that horse before we get home."

Casey unwrapped the fur from her feet and shook the snow out. From the gunnysack on his saddle Pinky took a roll of rawhide lacing and tossed it to her. "What d'ya know! It didn't even bust the jug. Save some of that rawhide so I can tie this here looking glass proper."

She had expected another protest about the mirror, a really violent upheaval. And she would not have blamed him, either. It was funny the way he had stood there, with the lining of her cape tied around his head edged with snow, with his eyes wide and startled as he felt his leg, after all that yelling about it being broken.

The frightful cold soon took the edge off her humor, starting when she felt the coldness of the saddle after mounting.

As far as Casey could tell, they never entered the valley she had seen from the summit, or at least they never got very far into it, for the hill was always there close by on her left side. The whiteness was a thick pall around them as they followed the road above a frozen creek that gurgled sullenly. Between the ice jams against dark rocks, the swift water was clear and clean. She loved bright, flowing water. Many times in the hill country of Missouri she had bathed in little runs, always to the great embarrassment of Billy Carpenter.

"Is there a river at your father's ranch, Mr. Bragg?"

"Heck, no. We got some springs."

They were in a canyon then where stark rock walls rose on both sides—cold, fractured stone with fir trees hanging ghostly, all clumpy with the thickly falling snow. They crossed a bridge. Pinky's horse snorted and made it in two nervous jumps when it felt the hollowness underfoot.

Then they were close to a big log building with a tight cluster of other buildings beside it. Light shone dimly through windows that were brittle-fringed with long icicles hanging from the eaves. Casey heard the sound of men's laughter inside and caught a glimpse of flames in a huge fireplace. All at once she realized how tired and cold she was.

Her mind denied the last three years. The log building was her family home in Illinois. She could run out of the cold into the warm kitchen and find her mother at the stove, her sisters setting the table in the lamplight, and her brother standing by the woodbox. It was a powerful vision and close within grasp. It seemed so simple to go inside, to warm by the fire, to eat hot food, and then to sleep and wake to a world unchanged.

Pinky's horse turned toward the building, and the bay followed it eagerly, but the man sawed the sorrel's head around savagely. They went on, past the warm light, the human sounds, on into the storm. Casey's vision vanished like a light suddenly dead in her mind.

"What was that place?" she asked.

"Just a way station."

"Why didn't we stop there?"

"Because I'm running things, and I didn't want to stop, that's why."

"But it's getting dark."

"I never figured the nighttime would bother you none. We got plenty of time to get where I'm going."

The snow never relented.

After they left the way station, they climbed steadily, first among shrouded fir trees and then in more open country where leafless aspens stood in scattered groves. After a time Casey realized that they were no longer following a road or even a trail.

She lost all track of place and time. She seemed to be drifting through a still, unreal world that had no problems any longer. Her horse followed the other horse without direction or urging. All she had to do was sit and feel the surge and fall of its shoulders and listen to the swish of snow against its legs and watch the smoke of its breath drifting to the side.

Altogether, it was a rather pleasant sensation, she thought.

She was jarred from her dreamy feelings sometime

46

later.

"What's the matter with you?" Pinky yelled. "Get off and bring him over here."

Casey looked at him numbly. He was dismounted, leading his horse toward an open-faced pole shelter that leaned for support on one end against a big pine tree. Casey felt herself leaning to match the slant of the shelter. It seemed funny to do that.

"Get down!" Pinky yelled.

Pushing against the saddle with both hands, she got her right leg over the cantle on the second try, and then she fell out of the saddle when her left leg would not bear all her weight. Her foot caught in the stirrup, and the bay dragged her halfway to the shelter before the foot came free. She lay on her back in the snow, almost content to stay there. It was the snow falling steadily against her face that made her realize she had to get up.

She rolled over and pushed herself up slowly. "What time is it?"

From somewhere in the lean-to Pinky answered irritably, "What the hell's the difference what time it is! Go in and get a fire started."

A fire? Casey hadn't even seen the tiny cabin, its roof plump with snow. She struggled over to the slab door and pushed. It resisted her until she found a crude wooden catch and shoved it back, and then the door swung in and she fell on her knees inside. For a while she could not see anything, but she could smell the mustiness of the place, rank with the odor of rats.

There were no windows. As she felt her way along the dirt floor, light came in from the whiteness outside and her eyes adjusted to the gloom. She saw a pole bunk littered with pine needles with a rat's nest in one corner of it, a small fireplace in the far corner of the room, and a cellar opening in the back wall, its door pushed outward by the weight of ice crowding into the room.

She got to the fireplace and was standing there numbly when Pinky came in, dragging a heavy stump. "Take some of those sticks out of that rat's nest and kindle the fire," he ordered. He got down on hands and knees and dug an ax out of the rat litter under the bunk. He began to chop pieces from the stump.

Casey didn't move.

"You all right?"

"Yes, I'm all right." It made Casey angry to know that for a while she had been almost helpless, not even thinking clearly. Her fingers did not respond well as she gathered sticks from the jackstraw pile of the rat's nest and carried them to the fireplace.

"What's the matter?" Pinky asked. "You act like something was wrong with this place."

"Oh, it's just fine." A stinking, rat-fouled, crumbling hut in the middle of nowhere!

"We're out of the storm, ain't we? Soon's I get a fire, it'll be real cozy." Pinky glanced at the bunk. "Yes, sir, real nice and cozy."

Casey tried to remove her scarf, but her fingers were not up to untying the knot under her chin. She clenched her hands, exercising them until the increased flow of blood made them tingle, and then the tips of her fingers began to ache. She untied her scarf, but when she tried to take it off, she found it frozen to her hair.

That seemed like the last straw. What in the world had she been thinking of to get into such a mess? The fire was beginning to crackle and blaze. She saw the crusted filth on the sticks she had handled, and as the flames grew, throwing light around the room, the primitiveness of the place became more apparent. Why,

48

it wasn't much better than the rat's nest she had robbed!

The light glinted on the mass of ice choking the cellar. She wondered if it would all melt when the room warmed up, if it ever did, and flood the floor.

"Now she's beginning to go!" Pinky said. He rubbed his hands, squatted there by the fireplace, pleased with himself and the situation. Again he glanced at the bunk.

Men, Casey thought bitterly. Drunk or sober, frozen, starved . . . morning, noon, and night . . . their minds were always on one thing. And this young hog was no exception.

She wondered if he would think of eating before making his clumsy play.

And then she wondered if he had even brought along anything to eat.

She was, as Miss Leduc would have said, in "a mood terrible."

# CHAPTER 6

*"I was sixteen when I walked in here behind a wagon, over Argentine Pass. For twelve years I was in the business here in Breckenridge. A woman was a damn fool to think she could get out of it and have a decent life any other way than by marrying a respectable man, so I did."* Long-retired madam, Breckenridge, Colorado, 1927.

CASEY'S VIEW OF THE SITUATION BRIGHTENED considerably after the fire warmed the cabin. It was a smelly, filthy den, but they weren't going to stay in it forever. Pinky laughed at her fear that the ice in the caved-in cellar would flood the floor. "That'll be there

49

until next summer."

In town he had been unsure of himself, but now he was confident and full of energy. He chopped the stump into firewood. He burned the rat's nest. From under the bunk he dragged a three-legged stool and arranged it near the fire for Casey to sit on. "Now you just rest yourself and get good and warm." He bustled over to the door and looked out. "She's still coming down hard." Pinky seemed pleased about the storm.

"Will the horses be all right?"

"Oh, sure. Don't worry none about them."

The tilted lean-to out there in the snow was a far cry from the big, warm barn where Casey's father had kept his horses, or the ornate stables at Schlottmeyer's Riding Academy back from the bluffs in St. Louis, where she had spent many an afternoon riding with gentlemen friends, but so was this cabin a great change from the habitations she was used to.

Horses and women just had to get used to the difference, she thought.

"You've used this place before, Mr. Bragg."

"Lots of times. Pa and us know a lot of places like this around the country."

I'll just bet they do, Casey thought.

"Where'd you get a name like Casey?"

"That's too long a story to go into tonight."

Pinky spread his hands to the fire. "Well, what'll we do first—eat or—"

He didn't finish. Casey gave him a steady look.

"Or get more wood." Pinky laughed nervously. He went out and came back with another stump, dragging in snow with it. "I rustled up some wood when the weather was good. It comes in handy. That's when I hid the ax. You got to hide things like that or people will

50

steal you blind."

"Oh?"

"You're danged right they will." Pinky plunged out again, returning this time with the gunnysack. He pulled out the jug and set it by the wall, and then he mined farther into the sack and came up with a handful of frozen meat strips well garnished with lint from the sack. He put the meat on a flat stone near the fire. "When that thaws a little, we can roast it."

Casey eyed the strips doubtfully.

"Most of that dirt will shake off," Pinky said. "A little dirt never hurt nobody nohow."

Though Casey needed no help with her scarf when she started to remove it, Pinky made a show of aiding her. "Gosh, you got pretty hair."

"Thank you, Mr. Bragg."

"No one hardly calls me mister. My name's Royal, but folks just call me Pinky. I . . ." He stroked the top of Casey's head. When she looked at him directly, he pulled his hand away quickly and went to the door once more. "Still coming straight down. Likely be two feet before morning."

"Will that make it impossible to travel?"

"Naw! A little snow won't bother us. We ain't so awful far from the place, anyhow."

"How far?"

"Five, six miles, maybe." Pinky hoisted the jug. "Shall we have one before supper?"

"No, thank you."

"What? I thought all you—I mean, you don't want a drink?"

"I don't drink." Casey paused. "Do you?"

The question took Pinky by surprise. In fact, it called a bluff, Casey decided. His expression turned sulky. "I drink whenever I please."

"Do you want to right now?"

It almost worked, but the youthful bravado in Pinky carried him on. He rested the jug on his shoulder and took a deep drink. His eyes watered as he swung the jug down. "That's pretty fair stuff, I'd say."

"Wasn't it awful cold?"

Pinky wiped his mouth with his hand. "Sort of, in my belly."

"You can hurt your insides, Mr. Bragg, by drinking in real cold weather. Whiskey won't freeze, you see, so it gets so cold it's harmful to take unless it's warmed up a little."

"Where'd you hear that?"

"I thought anyone knew that."

Pinky felt his stomach. "I don't feel no cold now. You're just trying to stop me from having a drink, is all."

Casey shrugged. "Help yourself. It's your stomach, Mr. Bragg." It would help some if she could keep him away from the jug. He was trying to work up his courage. She had him tagged accurately, she was sure— a young hog, a back-country lout who had never had a woman. His knowledge of women had been gained in talk behind the barn and from listening to older men boast.

He was determined to prove himself, and thought the whiskey would help. If he had not seen her when she got off the train and had not heard the man-talk about her, he would be no problem at all. But he had seen and heard. His judgment of her, she acknowledged bleakly, was a judgment that she would very likely spend the rest of her life overcoming.

Pinky felt the jug with his hand. "By gosh, it is a little

cold." He put it near the fireplace.

His eyes were bleary already, and he was blinking like an owl. He was a man who could not tolerate whiskey at all, Casey decided, but she had known some like him who had spent a lifetime trying to prove otherwise.

"You're a little bit scared of me, ain't you, Miss Casey?"

"You are an unusual sort of man, you know."

"I— How do you mean?"

"The way you handle things so well. You came through the storm right to this place without any trouble, and you knew what to do once we were here."

"Yeah." Pinky thought about it. "Yeah. Not everybody could do that, but I know this country." He strode over to the door and gave the storm more professional appraisal. "Still coming down. Looks like a good one."

What was good about a snowstorm, Casey wondered. "Tell me about your folks, Mr. Bragg." She watched him gathering pieces of fat pitch. He fed the fire, and then he stood leaning against the stone chimney. "How does your mother like it here?" Casey asked.

Pinky shook his head. "She don't much care for it. She says it ain't no place to raise girls."

"How old are your sisters?"

"Lemme see." Pinky contorted his face. "Cally is three years younger'n me, and Ella is a year younger'n her. That makes them fifteen and sixteen."

Then Pinky was nineteen, a year older than Casey had estimated. Her own age. It was hard to believe that this gangling, pinch-faced boy with the untidy smudge of beard had been in the world as long as she. "Were you born here—here in the hills?"

"Naw. We come here when I was four. How old are you?"

"Twenty-five."

"Yeah. That's about what I thought. Where—"

"How do you get along with your sisters?"

"I don't pay 'em much mind. They're all right, I guess." Pinky shrugged. "We get along pretty good, since they started growing up. What's all this talk for about my folks?"

"I'm just interested, that's all." Casey moved away from the fire. "It's warm enough in here now, I must say." She removed her jacket, and then the ragged woolen sweater under it, and then the two flannel shirts of Jensen's. Heavy clothing always made her feel uncomfortable. She untied the mink hides from her feet and hung them on a limb knot protruding from a log, wondering what old Mr. Winters would say if he could see them now.

Her hair was straggling. As she worked it in place as best she could, her hands brushed the ridgelog just above her head. The bottom of her blouse worked up. She tugged it down, pushing it inside her belt. If Ma Jensen's husband came home tonight, he wouldn't have much to wear, she thought wryly.

Pinky's mouth was half open as he leaned against the fireplace, looking back across his shoulder at her. Suddenly he swooped up the jug and took a drink. "Ah! That sure does hit the spot."

It hit something in him, all right, for he went over to Casey and grabbed her clumsily around the waist. "How about a little kiss, huh?"

"Why certainly, Mr. Bragg. I think you deserve something for the way you've conducted our trip." Casey gave him a quick peck on the cheek. He stiffened

54

and fell back and grabbed the bunk post and stood there with a silly, startled expression. "Thank you," Casey said.

"Me?" Pinky mumbled inanely. He rushed to the door to survey the storm.

"Is it still snowing?"

"Yep. Horses'll be all right, I guess, if that roof don't cave in, but it's been there for years, so it ought to hold." He closed the door. "That ain't much of a door, the way it sags at the top. Well, I guess we'd just as well eat now." He pawed around in the debris under the bunk and found two long sticks. "Most of the time when I'm in the hills I cook a lot of stuff just roasting it on a stick. A funny thing, stuff cooked like that agrees with Pa better'n cooking it in a fry pan." He began to sharpen the sticks. "Boy, you're sure some kisser, is all I got to say."

"I imagine you kiss quite a few girls, Mr. Bragg."

"Yeah. When I have the time."

Casey did not smile. She had a fair idea of the confusion and turmoil bothering Pinky. "Those young ones have in them a wildness they cannot understand," Miss Leduc had said. Few of them were ever allowed to get past the bar in her place. Besides instability, they had another weakness she did not like—lack of a large and steady income to make them treasured clients.

Casey took the stick Pinky held out, and then she borrowed his knife and whittled away a few unhealthy-looking discolorations. They knelt by the fire, roasting the strips of meat. "Where'd you get this?" she asked.

"Stole it from Jug Ears. He robbed me on a deal, so I just took what was handy. It didn't get me even, by no means, but it helped a little." Pinky's voice was slurred. He shook his head as if to clear it.

Those two drinks of whiskey had hit him very hard, Casey realized. "How did he rob you?"

"He bought one of the horses I stole last night, the good one, and all he gave me was fifteen dollars and that stinking saddle that like to killed me this afternoon."

The way Pinky talked about stealing, it seemed to hold no more significance than breathing. Casey wondered if he even considered it wrong. Probably not. People had said that thievery with the Braggs was not a vice but a way of life.

That was their concern. She had no intention of trying to reform them; she anticipated enough trouble taking care of her own problems.

Pinky kept turning his face away from the heat of the fire, opening and closing his eyes hard. Suddenly he blurted, "How long was you in that place?"

"What place?"

"You know. That—that house in St. Louis."

To cover her startled, panicky feeling, Casey pulled her stick back from the coals and lowered her head to look at the meat. Then she said evenly, "What makes you say St. Louis, Mr. Bragg?"

"Jug Ears said—He was just talking—He said something about a highfalutin place in St. Louis or somewhere."

Oh, yes, Jug Ears, the windy world traveler. He'd made a great effort to impress Casey with the extent of his knowledge of everything there in Ma Jensen's place. Before the men, probably when he first saw her, he'd made a big fat offhand guess—and hit the nail right on the head, without realizing it.

"He was all wrong, huh?" Pinky said hopefully. "I figured he was just blowing off like he always does."

56

Pinky was ready to be convinced. He would do it himself with just the slightest urging from her. Casey was tempted to do it, knowing that he was at a critical turn where she could make him swallow almost anything she wanted him to believe.

But so was she at a vital crossroads. Deceit was a worthless guide to follow. Evasion—well, that was different. "Do I look like someone who has been in the kind of place you're thinking of, Mr. Bragg?"

"No! And that's what I told those loudmouths, too."

Evasion was now deceit, since Pinky was taking it as pure denial of fact. Casey tried to temper it a little. "If any woman had spent time in such a place, would she care to admit it if she was trying to change her life?"

Pinky thought that over for a while. "I guess not," he said vaguely.

Casey began to eat the meat. "This is very good, no matter how you got it."

"Dang that Jug Ears, anyway! If the whole hog had been handy, I'd a-took it, believe me. He couldn't have cheated Pa the way he did me, you bet. I remember one time . . ." Pinky forgot what he was going to say. He raked hot coals back from the flames and threaded another piece of meat on the spit.

His mind was fogged with alcohol, but his hands were sure and steady, Casey observed. He divided the meat evenly between them, down to cutting the last strip in two with his long-bladed, wicked-looking pocketknife. In spite of the lint, which burned off, and a few grains of embedded dirt, which did not shake loose, the meat was delicious. Casey could have eaten four times as much.

When he had finished, Pinky put his back to the wall and stretched his legs across the dirt floor. "I been doing

57

some thinking. You didn't give me no straight answer a minute ago, did you?"

"No, I didn't."

"Why not?"

"You hired me, Mr. Bragg, and I accepted, and I told you the terms of our agreement on the way. That's about all we need to remember." Casey paused. "Where's my mirror?"

"It's out in the shed. It ain't hurt."

"Good."

Pinky slumped, as if he were getting ready to doze. He was that way for a few moments, and then he jerked his head up.

"You just never did answer me outright, did you?"

Casey said nothing. She put more wood on the fire.

Pinky reached out and hauled the jug across his legs. "You don't want no drink, huh?"

"No."

"I do. You going to try to talk me out of it?"

"No."

Pinky hesitated, and then he took a long pull. Some of the fluid dribbled out the corner of his mouth and ran down through his smudge of whiskers. He put the stopper in the jug, smacked it with his palm, and sat staring at Casey with one eye closed. "Your looking glass is in the shed."

"You told me."

"I took real good care of it."

"I know. Thank you."

Pinky's head turned toward one shoulder, his hands fell at his sides, and his whole appearance indicated that he was done for the night. Casey relaxed. It was a relief not to have to skirmish with him. She tilted the stool back, careful of the one short leg that had begun to rot.

A cold draft ran against her back when it touched the wall, but the cabin was so hot now that a little coolness was welcome.

Her own tiredness, the warmth in the softly shadowed room soothed her. She pictured the storm outside, snow falling in the night on the endless run of a strange land. Was this the far place she had dreamed of long ago? How quickly the outward aspects of her life had changed when she stepped from the train in Cimarron!

Nothing in the situation frightened her. Maybe that had always been part of her trouble, she thought—she had never been afraid of anything she tried, before or afterward. And if impulse had betrayed her, she would waste no time in mourning past mistakes. She looked at Pinky. A week before she would not have given him a minute's time, and now her future, her very life, was in his hands. A tormented boy who wanted her so badly that he had knocked himself out with whiskey in a futile effort to overcome his fear of her.

She did not dislike him. She saw him for what he was. As the youngest male of a clan devoted to thievery, he no doubt felt the need to prove his manhood in various ways—stealing horses by himself, bringing a low woman to his brothers as a gift, and of course he needed something to talk about when he arrived. Probably he would rate his horse stealing first and his conquest of her second.

So far, he had stolen two horses. Casey didn't intend to allow him anything else to brag about.

Thawed by the heat, bits of dirt dripped from between the rough poles of the roof. The flames licked steadily at the rich pitch-pine wood. Some of the smoke dribbled up the blackened front of the fireplace and gathered in layers against the roof, and then it moved slowly toward the cellar. Casey supposed there must be an opening to the outside above the ice of the caved-in cellar.

She was dozing when the rustling under the bunk roused her. A rat came from the shadows and pattered boldly across the floor, almost brushing her shoes as it passed. With its long nose it searched out the rock where the meat had lain. It sniffed around the stone, and then it found one of the sticks that had been used as a spit. Casey watched in drowsy fascination as the animal handled the stick with its forepaws, nibbling the greasy end.

Then, standing on its hind legs, it preened itself before the fire, its belly all silvery in the light.

She did not see Pinky move at all until he lashed out savagely at the rat with his foot. His quickness was amazing, but the rat was quicker yet. It flicked away and streaked across the floor to refuge under the bunk.

Pinky cursed rats in general. "They chew up every-thing that ain't in a tin box."

"I thought you were asleep."

"I was thinking." Pinky rose. "You know what I was thinking? It's time for me and you to go to bed."

"You're right. I am sleepy, so I think I'll settle here by the fire and—"

"That ain't what I mean, and you know it. You can't get around me forever with that soft talk." Pinky grabbed her by the arm and hauled her up. "Don't give me no more foolishness. I've had all that I want."

His sudden wild surge from complete inertness took Casey by surprise. He was wiry-strong and determined as he wrestled her toward the bunk.

"No, Mr. Bragg." She tried to be calm.

"What do you mean, no! You're nothing but a fancy whore, and we both know it."

Casey caught the bunk post with one hand and swung them both around. They bounced off the cellar door and crashed against the wall. Bits of earth rained down from the dirt-covered roof. "Why, goddamn you . . ." Pinky said.

"I am not going to bed with you!"

"I'm not good enough, huh? I'll show you." Pinky grabbed her blouse at the neck and ripped it open halfway down.

She jammed her heel down on his instep, and then she butted him under the chin with the top of her head. He staggered back a step. She gauged the distance to a heavy piece of firewood, but when she jumped to pick it up, Pinky swung his fist and hit her in the forehead.

It was a glancing blow, but it knocked her to her hands and knees against the ice of the cellarway. For a moment she considered going on down and feigning unconsciousness, but she knew he was so aroused now that he would take her even if she were unconscious.

He tugged at her to pull her up, to draw her toward him. She tried then a trick she had used on her brother when they were roughhousing as children. She braced one foot against the wall and drove herself forward in a billy-goat butt. She felt her head hit Pinky's belt buckle and then go on to smash him solidly in the belly.

He grunted and sagged away from her, but he did not go down. She got the piece of wood then. He caught her hand before she could swing it and began to haul her toward the bunk. With hands and knees, clawing, twisting, she fought him as best she could. They struck the edge of the bunk and fell on it. Casey tried to wriggle out from under him.

He put his wrist across her throat. "By God, now we'll see!" With his other hand he tugged at her belt.

61

Casey was pushing at his face with both hands, gasping as his wrist crushed down against her throat. Then, suddenly, all the steam went out of him. He rolled over and sat on the edge of the bunk, gulping. He lurched up and staggered to the door and flung it open and fell out into the night. A cold draft rushed in. The fireplace began to pour smoke into the room.

As Casey closed the door, she heard him bumping against the cabin, and then she heard the deep, wrenching convulsions of his sickness. She straightened her clothes, putting on one of the flannel shirts over her torn blouse. Her hair was stringing down again. She put it in place.

She had known many men, but none who had ever come at her like Pinky Bragg. She had often wondered what she would do in such a case. Now she knew. But if he had not gotten sick when he did . . . There was a wooden button on the door. She turned it. Now! Let him stay outside until the cold drove some sense into his skull.

She waited. He made no effort to get in. After ten minutes or more she opened the door and peered out. He was braced against the corner of the cabin, his head resting on his arms.

"You'd better come back inside, Mr. Bragg."

Pinky groaned. "I'm sick. Gawd, I'm sick." He retched weakly.

Casey shut the door and left him. After another five minutes she looked out again. He was in the same position. She went out and helped him back into the cabin. He was a miserable, shuddering specimen as he sat by the fire, making moist grunts and spitting. She brushed the plastered snow from his head and shoulders.

"Whiskey don't agree with me," he groaned.

Though that seemed fairly obvious, Casey made no comment.

"Pa's worse than me. A couple of drinks unsettles his belly something terrible."

After a while Pinky stopped shaking. He got up and chipped some ice from the cellar with his knife, and then he sat down quickly and began to suck on the pieces. It seemed to help him. He looked at Casey directly, hangdog, miserable, youthful.

"I oughtn't to've done it. I wasn't so drunk that I didn't know what I was doing." Pinky shook his head. "I'm sorry."

"Let's forget it then."

"You ain't what I thought, Miss Casey."

"To you, I'm whatever you think I am."

That was too much for Pinky to unravel. He shook his head wearily. "You meant what you said, but I didn't believe you. I wanted to, but . . . It won't work."

"What won't work?"

"You going on with me to the ranch. Eldon and Harve —they ain't like me, I'll tell you. It won't work."

"But I want to go on. I made an agreement."

"They didn't, not Eldon and Harve. Boston neither. And Pa didn't."

Casey said, "Let's talk about it in the morning."

"It won't be a bit different then. I'll take you back to Cimarron, Miss Casey. You can keep the money, too."

Now he was her champion. She felt a surge of pity for him. He had failed all down the line in everything he'd tried, and he didn't want his father and brothers to know about it, but there was more than that to his determination not to have her go on. He was, she thought, thinking of her instead of himself.

She slept on the floor. Just once during the night she

63

roused, when rats scurried over her body. Pinky was stretched out on the other side of the fireplace. Casey put more wood on the fire and went back to sleep. The jumper and the sweater were over her when she woke sometime later.

Pinky was rebuilding the fire, shivering as he crouched at the hearth.

"Can't you sleep?" she asked.

"It's morning."

The room was dark, full of cold. Casey pulled the jumper against her chin. "How do you know it's morning?"

"I just know, that's all." Pinky took the gunnysack down from the ridgelog and produced some biscuits that looked like pale rocks. "We'll eat, and then we'll get started back. I done looked at the horses, and they're all right."

When the fire caught and threw light on Pinky's face, Casey observed that he didn't look too well. No wonder. She let him believe they were going back, until after they had eaten some of the hard biscuits.

"I can't go back, Mr. Bragg."

"You've got to. I told you last night."

"I'm going through with it."

"Pa didn't hire you. I did! He don't know nothing about the whole deal."

"Then we'll let him decide whether you did something good or bad."

"You don't get what I mean," Pinky protested.

"Yes, I do," Casey said. "Who runs the ranch?"

"Who runs—Pa does, of course."

"Don't you think he'll honor an agreement you've made if he thinks it's fair?" Casey had gone too far in a major gamble to turn back.

"I don't know," Pinky mumbled. He sensed that command had passed. His smart idea had backfired on him, and it scared him to think what might happen to him when they got home, and, most of all, what might happen to Miss Casey.

"I'm ready, Mr. Bragg."

Their breath made vapor blooms in the pale light of early morning as they kicked their way through two feet of snow to the lean-to. They saddled the horses. When they led them out into the falling snow, the sorrel tried to pull away and return to the shelter.

"I better warm your horse up a little before you try riding him," Pinky said. "I don't feel too good." In the same breath he added, "Pa's got a mean temper, so don't say I didn't tell you."

# CHAPTER 7

*"I seen that outfit once at a dance on the Powderhorn. The old man kicked the stove over during a political argument. The big plug-ugly one got in a ruction with two miners and beat hell out of them. The one with the mouthful of gold teeth run off with my girl in the buggy I'd borrowed to carry her to the shindig, and one of the others swiped a saddle. That was about all I ever cared to see of the Braggs."* Barney Shelton, cowboy, St. Johns, Arizona, 1931.

NOW IT WAS WARMER, BUT THE CONSTANT, STRAIGHT-falling snow was making the going more difficult all the time as they climbed over upward among spruce trees heavily weighted with their white burden. On some of the tree trunks Casey saw slash marks that appeared to have been made by an ax. She was impressed by the beauty of the scene, the dark blue-green of the trees, the pure white of all else amid a silence broken only by the sounds of the laboring horses.

Pinky had spoken very little since leaving the cabin. Once when he had stopped to adjust his cinch, he looked at her with a shamed expression and asked her not to say anything to Pa about his behavior the night before.

"Very well, we'll forget about it, Mr. Bragg."

"We can still go back."

Casey shook her head.

Pinky wiped melting snow off his whiskers and looked around glumly. He was not the hustling, confident lad he had been the night before. At least he was through drinking for a while, Casey thought, though he had brought the jug along.

The mirror was an increasing nuisance. Sometimes they had to pass so close to trees that Pinky was forced to shift it from one side to the other, and occasionally he had to hold it out in front of him to ride between close-spaced trunks.

"What are those odd marks on the trees?" Casey asked.

"Blazes. They mark the trail."

"I see." They didn't mark it very well, Casey thought; they were too far apart. She doubted that she could follow them. Even Pinky had to stop and peer ahead at times to determine the next turn. He seemed to take a little longer each time he paused to do that. Looking back at one such stop, Casey was surprised to see how fast their trail was filling in behind them.

Where the trail led up steeply between two tall pines,

66

Pinky's horse balked. He dismounted and led it, stumbling upward with the mirror under his arm. When Casey started to get down, he said, "Stay on him. Don't worry about that old bay."

In strong, digging surges Casey's horse made the hill and came against the sorrel. Pinky was leaning on it, panting, his face pale, with a whiteness around his mouth that made his beard look like smudged dirt. "This old sorrel, he's starting to play out."

"Are you feeling all right?" Casey asked.

"I ain't exactly ready to rassle no bears."

The deepening of the snow was an inexorable growth that began to worry Casey after a while. For long stretches through the timber both she and Pinky led their horses. Below the new fall was old snow, coarse and crusted, strong enough to hold human weight only for an instant before letting the foot down with a jar. At every lunge the horses broke through to their shaggy bellies.

Tripped by the crust below the soft surface, Pinky fell sidewise and lay on the mirror, his chest heaving. "We shouldn't ought to come this way," he gasped.

"My horse is stronger. Let me go ahead."

"I'll break the trail." Pinky struggled to his feet and went on.

There was little old snow in the open stretches, and there the going was much easier, but they were making slow progress overall, Casey realized. She had no idea of how far they had come. When she asked Pinky, he said about halfway.

On the next hill his horse went down and did not respond to his efforts to make it rise. Cursing in a monotone of desperation, Pinky began to twist its ears.

"No!" Casey said. "Let me try."

Her father had always said she had a way with animals given only to those with a genuine love for dumb brutes. She proved it now by coaxing the sorrel to its feet.

"Think you're pretty smart, don't you?" Pinky grumbled.

She ignored him, led her horse around the trembling sorrel, and went ahead to break the trail. Pinky let her do it without protest, and that was the beginning of his disintegration. When she looked back sometime later, he was returning the jug to the sack.

The idiot, she thought.

Pushing through the snow in the timber took a fearful toll of Casey's energy. After her first strong burst she found she had to rest after every ten or fifteen paces. Pinky caught up with her and went around her.

"The one behind ought to lead the sorrel," Casey said. "Since he's not as strong as—"

"I'll do the thinking!" The whiskey had given Pinky a quick boost in energy and authority.

But neither lasted for long. He floundered ahead until both he and the horse gave out and had to rest, and there he stood, panting, staring through the falling snow with a vague expression. Ahead was open country.

"Which way now?" Casey asked.

"We got to cross the ridge on the other side of the park."

Park? The word fell strange in Casey's mind. An expanse of snow with leafless thickets around it, and on beyond, but dimly seen through the storm, a long hill lying at right angles to their course. She went around Pinky, then mounted and rode to the foot of the ridge. He came on slowly, leading the sorrel.

Casey had a hard time leading her horse to the

summit of the ridge. There were shelving rocks under the snow, and she had to angle back and forth a dozen times before she reached the top. Though there was no wind on the summit, she grew chilled to the bone while waiting for Pinky. As far as she could see ahead lay only the screaming wilderness that Riley had talked about.

Pinky's mouth was hanging open when he came up to where she waited. Moisture from his heavy breathing was frozen on the wings of his sheepskin collar. "We'll follow this here ridge south a ways," he said, pointing.

Direction meant nothing to Casey. She was beginning to wonder if it did to Pinky. They followed the ridge, the horses balky, uneasy about the slippery footing. After a short time they came to a great face of shattered rock that blocked the way.

Casey looked quietly at Pinky. "We turn down here?"

He squinched his eyes as he looked stupidly at the barrier. "Yeah. We got to turn down here."

They had to backtrack to find a place to go down after their first attempt brought them to the edge of a cliff. Without snow, descent would have been impossible, for the horses slid on their rumps most of the way down.

With Casey still leading, taking Pinky's directions, they beat their way through an aspen grove where the snow was as bad as in the blue timber. Then they entered a thicket of junipers and spruce trees where fallen trees and tangled undergrowth made further passage impossible, and that was the final confirmation of what Casey had known for some time.

They were lost.

There was no use in berating Pinky about it. "We're headed right," he mumbled, "but we missed the trail about a mile back."

With that, he leaned over and began to vomit. Snow covered the back of his coat as he stood hunched over, hands across his stomach, making long, shuddering sounds.

Casey's disgust was more for herself than him. Of the many unthinking steps she had made in her life, this one took the cake. Lost in a blinding storm with a drunken boy. Of all the warnings she had received in Cimarron, none had mentioned the likelihood of this situation. No, everyone had been greatly concerned about her honor.

Her honor, such as it was, she thought wryly, was certainly no problem now.

Lost, they surely were. Afraid, she was not.

Her right foot had been getting cold. She kicked snow off a fallen tree and rested her shoe on it to inspect the hide binding. The mink skins had been worn through. She adjusted the furs on both feet so that they were snug again. If she had to walk over another rocky ridge, they would be gone again. "How far now to your ranch, Mr. Bragg?"

Pinky lurched over to a tree and leaned against it. Snow cascaded down in a fluffy mass over his head and shoulders. "Not far," he muttered. "Couple of miles."

"What direction?"

Without moving his bowed head he pointed straight on into the tangle, an almost uncontrolled gesture that held direction only for an instant before his arm fell loosely. He retched and groaned.

"We'll build a fire and stay here until you feel better."

"I lost the looking glass."

"Where?"

"Coming off the ridge. I'll get it in a minute."

"I'll get it. You stay here and build a fire." Casey looked at Pinky doubtfully. "Do you understand? Build a fire."

"Yeah, yeah, all right!"

Before leaving she tied the horses to a tree.

Retracing steps already taken soon impressed her as a frightful waste of time and energy, but she would not quit. Although the trail was broken, her strength was a great deal less than it had been a few hours before. It took her much longer than she had thought to wallow through the aspen thicket and climb part way up the ridge, where she found the mirror near one of the long slide marks made by the horses.

It took her even longer to struggle back with it.

There was no fire. The sorrel horse was still tied where she had left it, and her carpetbag was lying in the snow.

Pinky and the good horse were gone.

She called his name. He had gone on ahead to better shelter under the trees to build the fire, she thought. There was no answer. She walked ahead a few steps before she realized that she was fighting unbroken snow. The only marks in the thicket were those they had made when entering and after dismounting.

She went back to the horse, looking carefully all around her—and completely overlooking the obvious. It was uncanny. It could not be. It seemed that some strange power had swooped Pinky and the horse aloft. For the first time that day fear and a touch of panic rose in Casey. She wondered if the cold and the exertion had addled her senses.

Once more she looked slowly around the grove.

And then the answer came, so simple that she slumped with relief. Pinky had left the grove the same way they had entered, and then he had turned off somewhere on the backtrail. She had been so intent on returning to the grove with the mirror, thinking of the comfort of a fire, that she had not noticed any marks other than the trench she was following.

She put the handle of her bag over the saddle horn, but she had nothing with which to tie the mirror on the horse, so she carried the heavy bundle. It seemed to have grown in weight during the past few minutes. Leading the weary sorrel, she backtracked and found where Pinky had turned off the trail, skirting around the grove.

The trail took her across the edge of a bog where the hoofs of the horse came up black with mud that gave off vapor before it froze. She came to a caved-in cabin with the tops of bushes showing above the snow inside the leaning walls. She rested there for a short time, looking at the ruins. She knew she could not rest too long any-where, for the trail was smoothing in with snow. Pinky's horse was strong, and it was going home.

Before long she knew she would have to abandon the mirror, but she was going to carry it as long as she could. In the silent gloom of falling snow she went on. The broken trail helped some, but her stride was not the same as Pinky's horse; where old snow crust lay below, she found herself more often impeded than helped by the holes the animal had made.

Her stops to rest became more frequent. She was tempted to leave the mirror and ride the sorrel, pushing it on with everything it had left. But it didn't have much left. She would lead it then, breaking trail until her strength gave out, and then she would demand the last of the animal's strength and courage.

She wished she had taken some of Pinky's matches.

At times in open country she thought the trail had disappeared, but it was only her eyes betraying her. She blinked the water from them and kept going, still clinging stubbornly to the mirror. At some point in the grinding struggle, she decided she would not give up the mirror at all.

She had no idea of how far she had gone when, on a hill not nearly as steep as many she had climbed that day, she discovered that the sorrel had more strength than she had thought. Halfway up the hill she leaned against the horse to rest, with her lungs burning and her legs trembling with the poisons of fatigue.

The horse showed a sudden surge of energy and started on. Casey grabbed a stirrup and let the animal pull her, staggering, to the top of a hill. Its ears were cocked ahead. It kept on going.

She knew why the sorrel had come to life when she saw the other horse fifty feet ahead. Pinky was lying on his back in the snow, the reins looped around his wrist. He grinned at her foolishly when she came up to him. "I been waiting for you, Miss Casey."

"Waiting! Why, you—" Her relief at finding him, coupled with a quick concern about his sick, helpless look, cut off her angry rebuke. "Get up, Mr. Bragg."

Pinky rolled his head. Snow was melting on his face. The front of him was covered with it. "Froze my guts with that drink of whiskey. Froze 'em something terrible, I did."

"You got sick to your stomach, that's all. Get up!"

"You don't need to get so mad. I'm sick." Pinky rolled over. He got on his feet, and then he fell on his face, driving his arms deep in the snow. His hat with the snakeskin band rolled away. He tried to crawl toward it, mumbling, spitting snow.

Casey was appalled at her own great weariness as she pulled him to his feet. Her first thought had been to

73

make him walk, but now she saw that he was in no condition to do that. If she put him on the good horse, he would run off again, unless she led it, and she was in no condition to do that.

She half-carried him to the sorrel and made him lean against it while she got her carpetbag down. "I can carry your old looking glass," Pinky said. "I got it this far, didn't I?"

It was a fight to get him in the saddle. He was loose weight without direction, though at the last moment he made an effort and helped haul himself in place. He leaned over the horn, chewing his protruding tongue, rolling his head with his eyes closed.

"Can you stay there?" Casey asked.

"Ride anything, for money, marbles, or—" Pinky slumped sidewise and began to fall. Casey tried to push him upright again, but he came down on top of her and knocked both of them into the snow. "Awful mean horse," he muttered.

"I'll kill you!"

"Yeah, 'at's a good idea, Miss Casey. Let's both do it."

"You drunken fool!"

"Ain't drunk, lady. Sick. Froze my guts."

Casey's anger gave her new energy to get Pinky on his feet again, but when she tried to boost him up, he could not swing his leg over the cantle. He fell across the saddle on his belly. Casey tied him there with his own lariat, using the rest of the stiff manila to lash the mirror on top of him.

He kept groaning for her to give him his hat. He could not do anything without his hat, he said.

"It won't stay on!" Casey yelled. She brushed the snow off her scarf and jammed his hat on her own head.

74

The bay horse had better know the way home, she thought. She wiped the snow out of the saddle and mounted. She hoped she had tied Pinky well enough to hold him in the saddle and that the sorrel had sense enough not to knock his brains out on a tree, and strength enough to go as far as they had to go.

The bay moved out readily enough, while the sorrel, with Pinky moaning about his lost hat, came along behind. It seemed to sense they were all somewhere close to better things.

Casey was not so sure about that herself. She let the bay have its head. After a time Pinky's protests trailed into silence. She rode back to look at him. His mittens had fallen off, and his hands were hanging limp and red. They would not be that color if they were freezing, she thought, but she was not sure that she was right.

She leaned down and felt one of his hands. It seemed to be as warm as her own; that is, she felt no appreciable degree of either heat or cold. Chapped and callus-rough, his hands were surprisingly small, long-fingered.

He stirred a little when he felt her touch.

It was growing late, or else the storm was thickening, for it seemed much darker when Casey peered ahead into the falling flakes for some human guidepost. There was nothing she could see but the snow, the hills, and the trees. All at once it seemed much colder, too.

She doubted that Pinky could remain much longer bound across the saddle without freezing his hands and feet. She recalled Old Roger, the Desbiens' coachman, whose hobbling walk on toeless feet was painful to watch. The tip of his nose was a grotesque smear, and there were seared patches of red on his cheekbones, all because he had lain drunk one night beside the stable in bitter weather.

When she let the bay go on again, she began to make plans for spending the night in the snow. She would risk another half hour's travel, as close as she could guess it, and then find someplace among the trees where she would try to make a camp.

The bay was moving strongly down a gentle hill among aspens when the buildings seemed to spring like magic out of the snow. Casey saw the outline of a corral, with white-backed cattle huddled in one corner, a barn that looked enormous, and the dark line of what seemed to be the top logs of a hog pen.

A moment later she heard the raucous gabble of geese warning of her approach. Then two huge dogs exploded out of the very earth in front of her horse, which paid their barking scant attention as it pushed on toward the barn. So intent was she on looking beyond the barn for a house or cabin that she rode between two buildings before she realized they were there. They were hard-set into the hill, and their roofs were covered with snow, so that from the back they had appeared to her bleary vision as part of the slope itself.

She stopped the horse and called out.

The door of the building on her right opened slightly. She saw a rifle barrel and caught a glimpse of a man's face, and then the rifle was withdrawn and the man rushed out. He was tall, grim-faced, with a wild shock of red hair streaked with gray. His face was long, with hard, down-streaking lines. He looked like a picture she had seen of John Brown with a saber raised on high, the fire of bitter dedication flaming across his features.

His voice was a roar of anguish. "Oh, my God! My boy, my little boy! Who shot him?"

Casey started to say that Pinky was not shot, but Joel Bragg bellowed again. "They'll pay in blood for this

76

day!"

Three other men had come from the second building and were plunging through the snow, the first a burly, dark-haired brute of a man. That would be Eldon, the ape, Casey thought, She caught the flash of a gold tooth in the mouth of one of the others. Harve.

At least I've reached the Bragg ranch, she thought.

She got out of the saddle on the second effort, sliding down while she hung to the horn to keep from falling. When her feet crushed into the snow, she was content to rest, trying to gather strength and will for the next step.

"What the hell is this thing on top of him?" someone said.

Casey watched them untie the mirror and toss it aside in the snow.

"He's alive!"

"Where you hit, Pinky?"

Pinky groaned piteously.

"Look at that frozen puke on him. He's drunk."

"Drunk?" the father yelled.

"It sure looks like it, Pa. There's a jug in this here sack, and—"

"The ingrate! The hound of hell!" Pa roared.

Pinky's brothers had untied him and were preparing to lift him off the saddle. Pa shoved them aside and grabbed the collar of Pinky's sheepskin. He gave it a mighty yank and dumped Pinky headfirst into the snow. "That any son of mine should be a drunkard . . . Look at him! Look at him laying there like a peach-orchard boar!"

So far they had paid little attention to Casey. Carrying her carpetbag, she went over to the mirror and picked it up, almost falling before she got it under her arm.

"Now just who the hell are you, son?" Pa asked.

77

"Casey Leclair." She saw that she had not conveyed anything with the name. She dropped the carpetbag, threw Pinky's hat in the snow, and pulled the scarf from her head.

"A woman!" Harve said.

"Well, by God!" Eldon yelled.

Casey grabbed up her bag again and marched toward the door where Pa had emerged. The other building, she guessed, must be a barracks for his sons. At the door she looked back. They were all coming toward her, all but Pinky, who was scrabbling around weakly in the snow where Pa had spilled him.

"I'm the cook. Pinky hired me," Casey said defiantly. In her desperation she tried to find support in the utterance.

They seemed to be coming at her like fiends. Harve was foremost, a smirking grin on his face. And the great, bull-shouldered Eldon, with dark hair low on his forehead, looked like a thirsty dog that has just spied a watering trough. "Some cook!" he whooped. "Did you see that wiggle, Harve?"

Casey wanted to leap inside and shut the door, but she faced them where she was, holding the mirror across her body.

"Hold up there," Pa growled.

His sons stopped as if they had struck a solid barrier. Pa shoved his way between two of them. "Take your sot of a brother to the bunkhouse. Look after the horses. I'll see about this cook business."

The boys hesitated, watching Casey.

"Get around!" Pa roared.

They moved then with alacrity.

# CHAPTER 8

*"Don't swallow none of those tales about her being so pious. She was high-priced, I know, but she was no saint. She lived with the Braggs quite a spell— how long, I don't recollect exactly. No young woman staying around them could have been straight. Or an old one, neither."* Caleb H. Penfield, Lake Fork homesteader, Powderhorn, Colorado, 1928.

"AND NOW, MISS FANCY BRITCHES, I WANT TO KNOW how you wound up here," Pa said. He was sitting at the long plank table in the house, a table littered with dirty dishes and pans, with food scraps stuck to the oilcloth, a box of cartridges, an asafetida bag, a Bible, a sheepskin coat with a scorched place in the back, and other items. His elbow tipped a frying pan with a half inch of congealed grease in it. He shoved it away roughly.

Casey began her story sitting down, but the room was so hot she felt the sickening swirl of nausea. She rose and stood behind her chair. The odors of sour clothing, old cooking, and general uncleanliness added to her queasy feeling.

"So he hired you, huh? What did you do to give him the idea—marry the idiot?"

"No, I didn't marry your son, Mr. Bragg."

Pa stared at her harshly. He would be a hard man to lie to, Casey thought—not that she had any intention of trying to fool him.

It was a big room, she observed. She could tell by the corners and along the walls that it had been rigorously scrubbed with lye many times, but now the floor was covered with mud and dirt and bits of manure from careless boots. The black stove was filthy with spilled grease, and the ash pan was running over on the floor.

Casey saw a pillared clock on a shelf across the room, the hands stopped at a few minutes before nine.

"Why'd you get off the train at Cimarron?" Pa demanded. In the way he squinched one eye, glowering through his bushy brow, he reminded Casey of Pinky.

"I was looking for work."

Pa grunted. "What kind of work?"

"Honest work, Mr. Bragg."

"You passed a lot better places to find it than where you stopped."

"I didn't know that."

Three doors led to rooms at the back of the cabin. Only one was open, showing a wooden bedstead with a gun belt hanging on the post. The bed was made, Casey observed, not neatly, but at least pulled together in rough order.

"You're standing there trying to make me believe you swallowed Pinky's story?" Pa said.

"I took his offer in good faith, yes."

Pa shook his head. His green eyes were hard and full of suspicion. "You ain't that dumb, sister. What did you say your name was?"

"Casey Leclair."

Pa snorted disgustedly. He dragged her bag over to him with one foot and began to rummage through it.

"Get out of that!" The heat was making Casey deathly sick. She tried to snatch the bag away from Pa. Without looking at her, he knocked her away with a casual sweep of his arm, back against the door. She felt the coldness flowing through the cracks, and it was like a

80

breath of life. Never before in her life had she fainted, but she knew she was going to if she didn't get out of the heat.

She pulled the door open and gulped the freshness.

"Shut that door," Pa growled.

"Close it yourself." Casey went outside and stood on the step. It was almost miraculous the way her nausea vanished, and then the cold began to gnaw at her. The storm was thinning down to small, hard particles of snow. From the building on the left, she heard loud laughter. The barracks boys. Apparently they were not worried about Pinky.

She went back inside, leaving the door open. Pa was stuffing her belongings into the carpetbag. He held up a vial of perfume. "No decent woman looking for work needs that." He dropped the vial into the stove.

"You have no right—" Casey grabbed the lid lifter. It burned her hand, and she dropped it on the floor. The vial of perfume popped in a small explosion in the firebox.

"Soft-handed, huh?" Pa said. "Kind of puny, too, letting the heat get you that way."

"I brought your son home through the storm!"

"Yeah, and you got him drunk to start the whole thing."

"I did no such thing, Mr. Bragg!"

Pa eyed her sternly. He opened a long-bladed pocketknife. "I told you a minute ago to shut that door, Cissie."

Casey closed the door and stood with her back against it, eying the knife.

"That's better. When I say something, do it." Pa began to slash the binding around the mirror, throwing canvas and the blanket padding aside. He held the

81

mirror up. "Jehoshaphat! Where'd you steal that?"

"From a crippled old woman," Casey snapped.

"That's a fair beauty. It'd bring a good price in one of the sporting houses in Gunnison." Pa admired himself. "Always need a shave, it seems like." He paused. "Is that where it came from—a sporting house someplace?"

"No."

Pa set the mirror against the woodbox. "You sure didn't leave much in your war sack to make yourself known, Cissie Leclair." He sat down at the table.

"Casey, not Cissie, Mr. Bragg."

"Cissie, Casey, Fifi, Dollie—all the same. What's your real name, Cissie?"

"Harriet Beecher Stowe."

Pa's lips tightened. His stare was like old John Brown's poised saber. "You're a flip one, sure enough. Now I've had all I can stand of your lying. Who sent you up here?"

"No one sent me."

"Tell the truth, you spawn of hell, or I'll slap all the taste out of your mouth." Pa rose.

"Why, you bull-roaring old wretch! You sit in this filthy hovel like you think you're the lord of all creation, calling me names." Casey snatched up the greasy frying pan from the table. "You slap me and I'll crack this on your thick skull. No one but your son had anything to do with my coming here. And I don't have to give you my life's history."

Pa watched her calmly. The threat of the frying pan didn't bother him in the least. Just the barest hint of a twinkle touched his eyes as he glanced around the room. "It is a mite untidy, ain't it?" He sat down and folded his hands on his stomach. "And you're a mite feisty for a woman with a name like Cissie Leclair."

"Casey, I told you!"

"Wrong kind of name, anyway. How'd you get that bruise on your forehead?"

"I rode into a tree limb."

"Uh-huh. So you claim nobody sent you?"

"Yes."

"Maybe." Pa nodded bleakly. "What makes you so sure I'm going to let you stay even one night?"

"I'm not sure." Casey saw by Pa's reaction that he had expected her to flare up again.

"You got here through a storm. I guess if I say so, you can leave the same way."

The very thought of going out into the snow again gave Casey the horrors, but she shrugged and said, "Yes, I can leave any time you say, Mr. Bragg."

Pa scowled. "Don't be so agreeable. I ain't drove no woman out into a storm yet. So you say my drunken son hired you."

"He had one drink today that I know of."

"Yep. That's what I said, my drunken son." Pa clasped his hands behind his head and leaned back. "You made a deal with him, but you didn't make none with me, and I happen to own this here ranch, Miss Fancy Britches."

"I was told the Braggs honor their agreements."

Pa was interested. "Who said?"

"Mrs. Jensen, for one."

"That old war ax, huh? Well, well . . ." Pa looked Casey up and down. "Where'd you hole in last night?"

"At an old cabin."

"Fireplace in one corner? Pole shed by a big tree?"

"Yes."

"Overton's." Pa closed one eye. "What happened then?"

83

"We built a fire and stayed there."

"Don't act cute with me! You and that yellow hair and that pretty, innocent face of yours . . . And that half-baked boy of mine with an itch like a young bull. Did you give in to him?"

"No!"

"Hmmm. Did he try?"

"Yes."

Pa grinned. "Well, well! He may amount to something, after all. I was beginning to wonder. Now when Harve was his age, no woman—"

"Mr. Bragg, I came here to cook, and that's all. Pinky is aware of the fact. In case I stay, I insist that you make my position quite clear to your other sons also."

"By Ned!" Pa roared. "You sound like a Philadelphia lawyer. If you stay! You make it sound like you had the say of things. I'm the one that tells everybody what to do around here. You *insist*. Jehoshaphat and little red hellions!"

He was very touchy on two points, Casey decided—his authority and his honor. He respected someone who stood up to him, but she was in no position to push that method too far. His greatest weakness was that he was a man; there were many ways to pierce a man's defenses or slide around his strong bastions. Casey said, "Your authority is apparent, Mr. Bragg. I'd never question it, but since you're a man of honor, I also want my position clearly understood. You—"

"I'd be crazy to keep you around," Pa mused. "Maybe you did make Pinky believe you're the Virgin Herself, but that was child's play. You take Eldon and Harve—"

"That's exactly why I'm asking you to—"

"Shut up a minute. You got a tongue like old Ma Jensen, I swear. Yap-yip-yap until a man's ears are ringing." Pa looked around the room sourly, as if he had lost the trend of his thought. "You're so all-fired sure my boys are going to try to drag you off to the bushes first chance they get. You think you're prettier'n a little red wagon because you had to slap Pinky's hands a time or two. Woman, there's other things besides what you're worrying about." Pa frowned as he gave some thought to the other things, without great success apparently, for he added, "Yeah, they'll try to get at you, never fear. Sure they will."

He got up suddenly and pulled his sheepskin toward him, dragging a few dirty tin plates off the table. "There's some things I let my boys find out for themselves. I even learn a little myself watching what happens that way, so I'm not going over to the bunkhouse and give them a great big sermon." Pa donned the coat and went to the door.

"I'm going to think on this business, Cissie. Since you're here, you can stay overnight." Pa pointed toward one of the closed doors at the back of the room. "Now get some proper clothes on and let's see if you know how to boil water without burning it." He shook his head. "A cook. Hah!"

He went out. The door bounced back from mud on the threshold. As Casey closed it, she saw Pa ploughing through the snow toward the corrals.

A bellowing old tyrant, but maybe she could get along with him. His sons would be another problem.

Casey changed her clothes as quickly as she could. The room Pa had pointed out for her use, like the whole back of the house, was built into the hill. There was one small window in the side that faced the barn and another, covered by snow, in the back wall. Dust was on everything. The room's stale coldness from months of being unoccupied with the door closed made Casey shiver.

She was amazed to see expensive tweed material, in three different patterns, covering all the walls. Pinned to it were fashion pictures from magazines, the fashions at least five years behind the times. A dresser and two chairs, all homemade, showed good workmanship. Casey had never seen such wood, streaked with bright colors, mostly orange and purple.

Over her dress she put on one of Ma Jensen's long white aprons. She had taken it without Ma's knowledge, leaving in return her blue velvet gown. She gave only brief longing to a desire for a bath and a few hours' rest. The best she could manage was to comb her tangled hair and wash her face and hands in the big tin washpan on the stand near the kitchen door.

First, she scoured the pan with ashes and soft soap.

Even without Pa in it, the main room was a frightful mess. It would have to wait. About all she could do today was to present some kind of meal on a clean table with clean dishes. If Pa decided to let her stay, the room would look different by tomorrow night.

While snow was melting in a copper wash boiler on the stove, Casey explored the pantry. It lay behind the middle door—a large storeroom lined with boards, with a screened ventilator in the roof. It was stacked and jammed with cases of canned goods, sacks of flour, sugar, potatoes, dried onions, buckets of lard, hams, and other supplies—a veritable treasure room of food. She shook her head over three cases of "Theo. M. Driskin's Saleratus, Supreme Quality."

No ordinary householder ever bought baking soda in amounts like that. Casey wondered if the Braggs had bought anything in the storeroom.

A haunch of beef lay on a maple butcher's block, with a cleaver and saw that badly needed washing. Suspended by a hook near the block was a side of beef. From the evidence Casey had seen on plates and frying pans, the Braggs must have been eating nothing but fried meat. She decided it would not be wise to jar their gastronomic habits with a radical change on her first meal, but at least she would show that hard-eyed old John Brown bastard that she could boil water without burning it to a crisp.

In the boar's nest of a bunkhouse a large stove with ornate nickeled skirts was roaring over its bellyful of pine chunks. Manufactured in Memphis, Tennessee, and consigned to a saloon in Ouray, Colorado, the stove's journey west had been uneventful until one fine summer night when it vanished from a boxcar on the siding at Sapinero while a freight was waiting for the division superintendent's special to pass.

Supine in his bunk nearby, Pinky Bragg was recovering from his ordeal with no help or sympathy from his three stalwart brothers. While his health was of no concern to them, they were rather interested in his knowledge of Casey Leclair.

"Did she know I was here when she agreed to come?" Harve asked. One thing about Harve, he was unhampered by modesty.

"She knew we all was here. I told her that."

"How'd you happen to get drunk?" Eldon asked. His face was designed for pig eyes, but something had gone wrong; his eyes were big and wide-set, while his mouth was small and tight, like his nose.

"I wasn't drunk!" Pinky said. "I froze my guts."

"You what?" Harve said incredulously.

"You heard me. I had one little drink of whiskey after we left the cabin. It—"

"He means he sniffed the cork." Harve was thinking about changing his shirt, but he didn't have a clean one. They were all in a dirty tangle where he had thrown them under his bunk. Boston, however, had two clean ones that he had washed himself the day before.

"Oh! So you stayed at the old Overton cabin all night." Eldon rolled his eyes. "Tell us about that, kid."

"Stop calling me that!" Pinky said. "Yeah, we stayed there." It was a subject he wished he could have avoided.

Eldon and Harve grinned at each other. "Well, how was it?" Eldon asked.

"It wasn't like you're thinking."

"Why not?" Harve asked. "Don't tell us you twisted your feet and got all bashful and spent the whole night keeping the fire going."

Pinky shook his head. "She ain't the kind you're thinking."

Harve laughed. "Tell us how you found out, Pinky boy."

"Pinky boy yourself! I just know. I'm telling you I know, damn it."

Harve was enjoying himself. "We want to know how you know."

"I'll tell you," Eldon said. "He tried to put his arm around her. She yelled bloody murder, so he run like hell out of the cabin and slept in the lean-to with the horses." He smacked his fist against the palm of his hand and laughed uproariously. Pa always said Eldon's laugh was enough to stagger a bull at twenty paces. "Ain't that a fact, Pinky?"

"Go to hell," Pinky said sullenly. He wished he'd

never gotten the whole business started. If he'd watched her get off the train and then gone on about his affairs, he would have saved her and him a pile of trouble. At the moment he hated his brothers. He couldn't think of anything to help Casey.

Pa could handle things if he would, but you couldn't always tell about Pa. If he said she was hired, she'd get paid what Pinky had promised. That much was sure about Pa, but the rest . . . you just couldn't tell.

Having found tremendous humor in his version of what had happened at Overton's cabin, Eldon repeated the story, along with the laugh, and then Harve added some embellishments to make it even more interesting.

At a table in the middle of the room where the Bragg boys sometimes sneaked in a card game when Pa wasn't around, Boston was cleaning the chimneys of two railroad lanterns. He hadn't said much, except to ask Pinky how he was feeling.

A touch of red in Boston's hair was the only hint about him to mark him as Pa's son. His brown eyes were mild, his manner quiet, qualities which made people who disliked the Braggs—just about everyone— say that Boston must be a throwback of some kind, or maybe even a bastard calf. He was a solid man, twenty pounds lighter than Eldon, who tipped the beam on Joe Harbor's scales at 235.

Harve was about the same weight as Boston, three inches taller, with quick, whiplike strength and agility, but Boston was the one who could stay with Eldon in a roughhouse.

In the midst of some interesting speculation about Casey, Harve broke off to say, "Hey, look at old Boston there! You'd think he'd been living next door to a whorehouse, the way he's trying to let on. You and me

89

better watch him, Eldon, or he'll get there first with that sneaky thank-you-ma'am way of his. Women get fooled by that stuff, you know."

"Like you fooled the woman at Sapinero that time?" Boston asked.

Eldon whacked his fist into his palm and brayed. The incident Boston had referred to involved the whole Bragg outfit having to fight off a camp of railroad construction workers to save Harve's hide after he made a misjudgment of one of their women washing clothes in the Gunnison River. Harve had made a good many similar mistakes in his time, but his operating principle of never knowing unless one tried had struck a high enough ratio of success to warrant continued use of the pragmatic method. In the process he had acquired some knife scars and two minor bullet wounds, which he viewed with pride on the infrequent occasions when he bathed all over.

After his humor at Harve's expense wore thin, Eldon asked, "You reckon Pa is going to let her stay awhile?"

That was a sticky question. "It's hard to say," Harve allowed. "Pa has his ways, you know." Indeed he did, mighty tall ways in some respects. He was hell for saying grace at meals. He didn't allow cussing around women. If you gave your word, you had to stick to it, even if you'd given it to a Democrat or a man from Kansas. He didn't hold with stealing from Missourians. Once when Boston had said that maybe some Missourians held stock in the Denver and Rio Grande Railroad, Pa declared a railroad was a thing, not a person. Stealing from a "thing" was all right.

Yes, Pa had his ways, sure enough. At home he shaved every day, and his sons had to do the same. He was against gambling and against drinking more than an occasional snort to seal a bargain. Maybe that was because whiskey gave him a sour belly. He never said a thing about his boys enjoying themselves in a fancy house, but importing such fun right to the ranch . . . You just couldn't tell; he might take a real narrow-minded view of that.

In fact, Harve decided that was exactly what Pa would do, and that was a dirty shame, too.

Eldon was thinking the same way. "If she's only here for one night, we've got to figure a way to get around Pa."

"You didn't get up early enough this morning to do that," Boston observed.

"Even if you could fox Pa, it wouldn't do you no good," Pinky said. "She ain't that kind, I'm telling you."

"Just because she threw your ass out of that cabin— Wait a minute!" Harve was looking at the jug of Forty Rod they had found on Pinky's bay horse. "You're telling the truth, Pinky—you had just one little drink?"

"So help me. Made me sicker'n a dog. You drink whiskey out in the fearful cold and you don't think anything about it because it won't freeze, but it's way below zero sloshing around in the jug. You gulp down a drink and bingo!—your guts are froze up just like that. You can't do nothing."

Pinky's brothers gave the theory careful consideration. None of them could recall taking a drink of sub-zero whiskey, but old Pinky, coming home tied belly-down across a horse, had been fair evidence that such drinking didn't do a man any good.

"Just one snort, huh, and not even a big one?" Harve asked thoughtfully.

"I'll take an oath," Pinky declared.

"It sounds reasonable," Boston allowed, "but don't it

91

warm up in your mouth and on the way down? Looks like it would."

"I guess it would if you sloshed it around in your mouth before you swallowed, but I didn't do that. When you drink out of a jug, you're more interested in swallowing than anything else. Then there you are, with that whiskey strung out like a big icicle all the way through your insides." Pinky shook his head. "How'd you like to have a big long icicle in your guts and have to stand around until it thawed?"

"To tell the truth, it don't hardly appeal to me at all," Boston said.

"What's your idea, Harve?" Eldon asked.

"Real simple. We give Pa a royal gut-freezing."

"Yeah!" Eldon grinned.

"Pa won't take no drink on our say-so," Boston objected.

"Sure he will if we all have a couple, and he's a gulper, too," Harve said. He picked up the jug. "I'll just set this out in the snow—"

"We drink, too, huh?" Eldon said. "I don't want to freeze my guts." The vision of that great long icicle was not a pleasant one.

"Slosh it!" Harve said. "Better yet, stick your tongue in the jug and don't get any at all."

"I think I'll slosh. Pa's tricky. He might see my swallowing ain't real. Maybe we better all slosh."

"I don't know about this," Boston said. "Pa wasn't born yesterday."

"Neither was we," Harve said. "I say it'll work if we all act natural. Pa will be as sick as Pinky was. All we do is let him wander over here and go to bed. He always comes here when his belly is upset. Then we have ourselves a time with that little yellow-haired gal."

"Yeah!" Eldon grinned like a hungry wolf.

"Didn't you say it was the night before Christmas, Pinky?" Harve asked.

"Yeah," Pinky said glumly.

Harve showed his fine gold tooth. "How can Pa turn down a few snorts on the night before Christmas?"

"I've seen him turn down even one snort on Election Day," Boston said.

"I'll be first," Eldon said. "I'm the oldest."

"You might turn out to be the lumpiest, too, if she's like Pinky said." Boston grinned.

# CHAPTER 9

*"A lot of writing about the West is like the junk I read about the early days of baseball—baloney. Women, for instance. Sure they were scarce, but they weren't near as sacred as some of the yarns make out."* Emil Becker, former Pittsburgh pitcher, Turret, Colorado, Mining District pioneer; Turret, 1933.

PA CAME IN AND STOMPED THE SNOW OFF HIS FEET and put his sheepskin on the table. Casey picked up the coat and hung it on a peg at the far end of the room.

"Starting to run things already," Pa observed.

"I just washed that table, Mr. Bragg."

"So I see." Pat sat down. "We got a spring here. You don't have to make water by melting snow in a boiler."

"Where is the spring?"

"Just above the geese pen. There's a couple of buckets and a yoke somewhere outside. Real handy for carrying water."

"Are they?"

Pa was grimmer than cold stone for a while. "You don't strain anything to get along, do you, Cissie?"

Casey began to mix biscuit dough on the table.

"Takes a woman to turn a place upside down," Pa said. "I see you prowled into the pantry."

"It seemed the most likely place to find food."

"Sarcastic, too," Pa mused. "Them steaks you got there came from one of Ross Chamberlain's steers. There's another one butchered up nice and buried in the snow out on the hill." He never took his eyes from her. "You say you've never heard of old Ross or Stan Meixler or the Kimballs?"

"I didn't say so, but I haven't heard of them."

"Or Billy Armbruster, either?"

Casey went on with her work. "I've told you, Mr. Bragg, I don't know a soul out here."

"Yeah. I heard you say it, Cissie. Answer me something else. Did you ride free on the railroad?"

Casey dusted flour from her hands and faced Pa squarely. "I did not. You seem to think that someone sent me here to spy on you. You're wrong. For all I care, you can steal the courthouse of whatever outlandish county we're in, or an engine from the railroad, or all the horses between here and California. That's none of my affair. I came here only to cook."

"Hmmm," Pa said, "an engine." The idea seemed to fascinate him for a few moments. "That's the part that don't jibe, you coming here just to cook." He was genuinely puzzled, and it made him ornery looking. "Did you have some idea of turning my place into a tenderloin district?"

Casey wanted to bash him with something heavy. She was bone tired, trying to hurry to cook a meal under

94

strange conditions, and she knew her worst problems were still ahead. But it was a situation she had put herself into voluntarily.

"Did you?" Pa demanded.

She clenched her teeth and said, "No, Mr. Bragg."

Pa just stared at her, with his legs stuck out in the way, with snow melting off his boots into the mud and manure on the floor. "It didn't seem likely, but I ain't made up my mind about you, not at all."

His scrutiny made her far more nervous than she let him know. Once when she paused by the stove to flex her fingers, which had been hurting in the joints all afternoon, Pa nodded sagely and said, "Rheumatics, eh? How old are you?"

"None of your business, Mr. Bragg."

Pa didn't change expression. Later he said, "What the devil kind of way is that to ruin meat?" when Casey began to broil steaks in the oven.

"If you don't like the taste, I'll melt a cup of grease for that touchy belly of yours."

"Who said I had a touchy belly? Who said?"

"Ma Jensen, for one."

"So you asked everybody about me. Ma Jensen! One meal in her place and a bear would have a sour belly. I belched coffee for ten miles after eating breakfast there one time."

The oven door fell down when Casey tried to close it. She tried twice more before she discovered she had to lift it to make it catch.

"Ever use an oven before?" Pa asked.

She vowed he was not going to get her goat.

"Where'd Pinky get that horse you hauled him in on?"

As if Pa didn't know! "He said he stole it

somewhere."

"One horse ain't enough evidence for you, huh?"

"Forget that crazy idea, Mr. Bragg." Casey remembered to use a potholder before touching the stove lifter, having burned her hand twice that afternoon. She put the last of the sticks from the woodbox into the fire.

"Takes a heap of wood around here," Pa observed. "I filled that twice today." His attitude indicated that he did not intend to do so again.

Casey found it a relief to go outside and get away from him for a short time. It had stopped snowing. Dusk was coming, making a cold blue light on the snow. The air bit at Casey's cheekbones and fingers with tiny hooked claws as she gathered an armful of wood from the huge pile.

One of the Bragg boys laughed like a wild jackass in the bunkhouse. Pa had thought it very funny when Casey had called it a barracks.

"The meat's burning!" Pa shouted.

Casey hurried inside. It was not the meat burning; it was only smoke from the grease that had splattered outside the drip pan Casey had placed in the oven. Pa watched proceedings with an "I told you so" expression.

After a while he said, "It's getting sort of dark in here."

Above the table hung a large lamp, and in cast-iron brackets around the walls were six others, all with sooted chimneys. Casey agreed that it was getting dark and went on with her chores. Pa got up and lit the lamp over the table. "Wick needs trimming and the chimney's a fright." He sighed. "I don't know how she kept up with the work around here."

Casey was wondering the same thing about Mrs.

Bragg. Of course, she had two daughters to help her. The biscuits were about done. She set the table, working around Pa, who had resumed his seat. "We're ready to eat, Mr. Bragg."

"There's a piece of railroad iron hanging outside the door, with a banger. Just slam it a time or two and get out of the way quick."

The banger was a steel rod suspended by a rope. When Casey clasped it, her damp hand froze to it instantly. Once on a cold morning her brother had talked her into sticking her tongue to a wire fence, and she had jerked away and left a strip of flesh on the wire. It was a lesson she remembered, so now she resisted the urge to unclasp her fingers. Instead she gripped the rod tighter, holding on until the warmth of her hands melted the frost on the metal and allowed her to free her hand without injury.

It was just another irritating incident in a long list, but for a moment it was almost the straw that broke the camel's back. She took several deep breaths and pulled herself together. If she could just survive this first day . . . She protected her hand with her apron the next time she gripped the banger. The first clanging signal was still hanging in the icy air when the bunkhouse door flew open and out burst Eldon, Boston, and Pinky, charging through the snow like runaway caribou.

That Pinky, Casey thought, surely had wonderful recuperative power.

They made a noise like cattle crossing a shaky bridge as they stampeded in and plunked down at the table. Then all the chair-scraping and boot-dragging and grunting was done and there was a sudden strange quietness as they sat there with their hands in their laps like obedient schoolchildren.

97

"This here is Cissie Leclair, boys," Pa said. "I told her she could stay tonight."

"It's Casey, Pa, not Cissie," Pinky said.

"Shut up. Where's Harve?"

"I thought he was right behind us," Eldon said. "He—"

"All right. Shut up," Pa ordered.

They watched Casey putting food on the table. She knew Pinky, so she didn't have to size him up. Eldon confirmed her first impression of him—a big animal, a rutting buffalo. His neck was so short that the collar of his blue woolen shirt covered all of it. In fact, the first few buttons were missing, so that the shirt gaped open to show red underwear, also with missing buttons. With his tongue in the corner of his mouth he watched Casey with a big-eyed stare.

She had her first close look at Boston, too. If she had seen him apart from his family, she would have called him pleasant looking, rather handsome, but now he was just another Bragg removing her clothes with his stare.

Harve came in. His hair was plastered down with water, parted in the middle, with a hand-dented wave on the left side. "Good evening, Miss Leclair," he said, beaming his gold-glinted smile. "It's a pleasure to—"

"Shut up and set down," Pa said.

"So that's why you hung back—to get my clean shirt," Boston said. "You just wait until—"

"I'm getting tired of saying shut up," Pa announced. He pulled his legs under the table and scraped his chair in close. He cleared his throat, and his sons bowed their heads. "O Lord, we thank Thee for this food and for Thy blessings and for delivering my drunken son from the storm. Amen!" Whereupon Pa speared the largest steak on the platter, catching his sons with their heads still bowed and their hands dutifully folded.

98

"That was a mighty short prayer, Pa," Eldon complained.

"Warn't it just?" Pa said.

At the Desbien mansion while learning some of the finer skills of cooking, Casey had often worked all day helping prepare a supper that the Desbiens and their guests then spent two hours in consuming. She was aware that not everyone ate in such a leisurely manner, but never had she seen such swift and utter consumption of food as now took place.

The Braggs attacked the table as if they were holy avengers and the food the grapes of wrath. They spoke little, conveying their wants mainly by grunting. When it was necessary to point, they did it with one hand while lifting food to their mouths with the other. Casey had scarcely placed the last biscuit on the table before everything was gone, including a small steak that she foolishly had thought to eat later, but it did not matter; she was so tired the thought of eating revolted her, particularly after the demonstration she had just seen.

Pa dropped his knife and fork onto his plate with a clatter. That was the signal that the meal was over, that no one was to continue eating. It did not matter this time, because his sons had beaten him, anyway.

"We'll set a spell," Pa said.

Casey knew how they arrived and how they ate. The usual procedure, apparently, was to depart at the same tempo, but Pa was making an exception tonight. They sucked their teeth or picked at them with fingernails and stared at Casey as she gathered up the wreckage. No one commented on her cooking. Swill would have served them well enough, she thought.

Eldon said, "I just happened to think, ain't it the night before Christmas?"

"By gosh!" Harve said. "I believe it is."

"What do you know about that!" Boston said.

"Well, I declare . . ." Pa looked at his sons with an indulgent expression. "Ain't it a shame we don't have a big chimley for old Santy to come down!"

The room rocked with Eldon's guffaw, and then he rolled his eyes at Casey and all but licked his chops.

Casey grabbed the wash boiler and a cooking pot and went outside for snow. Pa Bragg could roast in hell before she carried water from a spring with a coolie yoke. Harve came out, with Pinky on his heels. As Casey stooped to dip snow into the boiler, Harve patted her bottom. She whirled around and threw the snow in his face, and then she tried to hit him with the pot.

He laughed and jumped back out of reach.

"You leave her alone," Pinky said. He helped Casey fill the wash boiler.

"You'd better get back to the bunkhouse, little boy," Harve said. "You had your chance and couldn't handle it."

"You just leave her be, that's all!"

Casey left them arguing and went inside. She slammed the boiler down on the stove, and snow fell off it, popping and sizzling on the hot lids.

"Doggone it, I told you we got a spring," Pa said. "You can bust the stove, dumping ice on it that way."

Casey began to scrape bones and crumbs from the plates into the stove. Pinky and Harve came in, Pinky with a worried "didn't I tell you?" expression as he glanced at Casey. Harve's long face was red with melting snow, but he wore a smirk that didn't change even when Pa grinned and asked him if he'd fallen down.

"It being the night before Christmas and all, we

100

figured a drink wouldn't do no harm." Harve held up the jug of Forty Rod.

"Yeah!" Eldon said. "How about it, Pa?"

"Hmmm." Pa looked at his sons like a benign old patriarch. "I don't know, boys."

"Aw, come on, Pa," Harve coaxed.

"It's the night before Christmas, Pa," Eldon said. "We ought to do something. It ain't hardly right not to celebrate just a little."

"Well," Pa said slowly, "I guess a snort or two won't hurt nobody."

Harve plunked the jug down in front of his father.

"I don't want none," Pinky said hastily.

"Didn't figure on letting you have any," Pa said. "Getting drunk twice in the same day is a little too much for a growing boy."

"I wasn't drunk. What happened was—"

"Shut up!"

Helpfully Harve pulled the cork for Pa.

"Hmmm. A lot of politeness around here." Pa hooked his thumb in the handle, swung the jug to his shoulder, and swigged away. "Whew! That do go down cold."

"It warms fast, though," Eldon said quickly. He and Boston and Harve all had a drink, sloshing the cold whiskey around in their mouths before swallowing cautiously. Almost before anyone could say, "Freeze your guts," the jug was back to Pa.

He took another big gulp.

Once more Harve sent the jug around. This time the boys tongued it and didn't get very much, except Boston, whose tongue slipped a little when he saw Pa watching him keenly. Boston strangled and gasped and wheezed, while Eldon laughed and thumped him on the back.

Pinky divided his attention between Pa and Casey, watching them in helpless desperation.

"Ain't you getting a little eager?" Pa said, when Harve thumped the jug before him the third time.

"Christmas, Pa. Merry Christmas!"

Pa had the third one. He put the cork in the jug and set it on the floor. "That'll do us all."

Between glances at Casey, the Bragg boys watched Pa. If Pinky was right, though baby brothers seldom were, that big icicle in Pa's guts ought to be working pretty quick. When nothing happened right off, Harve and Eldon began casting mean looks at Pinky.

"Well," Pinky said, "I guess we'd better be getting back to the bunkhouse, huh?"

"You go right along, Pinky," Eldon said.

"Stay here," Pa said. "I'll tell you what we're going to do tomorrow." He made tasting sounds, shaking his head. "No matter if we do have a big snow, that don't mean we're going to sit around like millionaires. We—" He made a face. "What kind of rotgut was that, anyway?"

"Real good stuff," Harve said. "Maybe another one—"

"I got enough."

"Yeah, Pa," Pinky said. "You see—"

"You shut up!" Eldon raised his arm.

"I'll do the shutting up around here." Pa said it, but he didn't have his usual force. He wasn't looking good at all. Suddenly the hiccups hit him. He got a stricken expression. "By Ned," he mumbled, and headed for the door. "I'm going over to the bunkhouse for a minute." He stumbled out, leaving the door open.

Harve watched in the doorway for a moment, and then he shut the door. "It worked! He's done for the night." He went over to where Casey was watching the

102

thumping boiler on the stove. "You can do those dishes any old time, girlie." He took her wrists. "You know, you're a real pretty one to be a cook."

Eldon shouldered his brother aside. "She don't need none of your smooth talk. What she needs is a man."

Casey had just put wood in the fire. She was still holding the potholder. She edged toward the woodbox to grab a piece of heavy pitch pine, but Eldon grabbed her around the waist and pulled her in tight against him. He had the strength of an ox and the odor of one, too. As he hunched down to kiss her, she jerked her head sidewise. "That's it, fight a little," he said. He slobbered all over her neck.

She had never thought that any man could frighten her, but she had never been mauled by anyone like Eldon Bragg. The press of his face against her neck, his tremendous strength, his brutal, overpowering lust sent shivers down her spine.

She knew that trying to fight him with physical force was useless. It would only excite him more. Across his shoulder she saw the other three Braggs. Pinky was looking on with his face twisted and scared. Harve was grinning. Boston was sitting at the table, merely watching.

The only help she was going to get was from herself.

She tried to twist farther away from Eldon. That was when she saw the stove lifter. Eldon scooped her up in his arms. At the same time she wrapped the potholder around the lifter and plucked it from the stove. She made no resistance as Eldon started toward the bedroom with her.

He stopped and turned to look back at his brothers.

"See there, Harve? I always did say you wasted too much time fancy-prancing. You fellows just as well go

103

see how Pa's getting along. Me and Casey here is going to be pretty busy for a long time!"

He was in the middle of his big laugh when Casey pulled his loose-fitting collar back and shoved the stove lifter down his spine, next to the skin. She crammed the potholder on top of it for good measure.

"Ahwoo!" Eldon bellowed. He dropped Casey like a hot potato and began to claw at his shirt. War-dancing around the room, he got his shirt off. His gyrations had helped work the burning metal on down his back to lodge against his belt. Still jumping in pain, he pulled his undershirt up and the lifter fell on the floor.

Until then his brothers, who had been watching in astonishment, didn't know what had happened.

"She put the stove lifter down his neck!" Harve howled. He pounded the table with his hands, laughing. Pinky and Boston began to roar.

For a moment it was touch-and-go with Eldon—Casey or his brothers. He decided his brothers were the greater irritant. Lowering his shoulders, he charged Harve and knocked him on his back on the table. Harve doubled his knees and kicked Eldon in the chest. His boots made a solid sound, but the impact checked Eldon only for an instant. "Laugh at me!" he shouted, and dove at Harve.

In trying to get away, Harve rolled off the table and fell into Boston's lap. "Right here is where I get my shirt back," Boston said.

Eldon went over the table after both of them. Three heavy bodies crashed against the floor in a grunting, threshing tangle of legs and arms as Boston's chair collapsed. Clutching hands pulled Eldon's underwear over his head. He punched someone, and someone punched him back. Boston yelled angrily when an elbow slammed into his eye. He struck out blindly with a piece of the broken chair and slammed Harve in the ribs.

They fought the way they ate, Casey thought. They tried to demolish everything they could reach.

Pinky had slid away from the table unharmed. He stood in the doorway of Pa's bedroom and yelled delightedly, "Slug him! Bust him!"

Outside, the dogs began to bark.

Casey had seen rivermen in horribly brutal fights. The Braggs were as bad or even worse, and their language was a fright.

Why, they were going to wreck the house, or kill each other, or both. The floor shuddered, and caked mud jumped upward from the cracks. The table tilted and then settled back with a hard thump. A chair skidded toward Pinky, who reached out with his foot to stop it.

"No fair gouging!" someone yelled from the melee of flailing legs and arms.

They had rules for that kind of disorganized mayhem? Casey shook her head in wonder.

Then Pa came stomping in with the yoke for the water pails. He watched the combat calmly for a few moments, sitting on one corner of the table with the heavy piece of oak across his legs. "That Harve always was a biter," he said. Someone's howl testified to the statement. Pa shook his head at Casey. "Never did see 'em in such a twist as that. I can't make out whose parts belong to who."

Eldon roared in pain.

"Yep," Pa said, "that Harve sure is a biter."

Pinky had a better angle of view. "Boston twisted his foot, Pa."

An instant later a boot came flying out of the tangle.

"Well, I declare . . ." Pa rose unhurriedly and began to lay about with the yoke. He struck heads, bottoms, ribs, shoulders, arms—any exposed surface that reared above the general level that his blows soon established—and then he whaled in a few more licks for good measure.

The combatants quickly rolled apart. The sounds of battle died. There were labored grunts and other sounds of anguish. Pa waved the yoke like a wand. "Ain't it awful, them trying to stun their poor old pa with a drink or two of whiskey! They must have thought I was borned yesterday."

No one cared to comment.

"Now get up and get out of here!"

They rose as quickly as they could, in various states of disrepair. Eldon's undershirt was in shreds. His skin was remarkably white, hairless, all the better to show an assortment of livid marks, including one on his biceps that was definitely the print of teeth. Boston held one hand over his eye. The other clutched the once clean shirt he had retrieved from Harve, at least the tattered remnants. Harve moved with some difficulty, feeling his ribs. His sleek hair was awry, and his nose was bleeding.

"Ain't you a fine-looking outfit?" Pa said. He brandished the yoke. "Move!"

They moved, fleeing into the night like big, ungainly birds disturbed from their roosts. One of the dogs howled as someone trampled it in the rush.

Pa looked at Pinky. "You, too."

"I'm going, Pa, I'm going."

It seemed that Pinky would escape scot-free, but when his course was well lined with the door, Pa swung a mighty stroke against his backside and sped him on his way.

Pa kicked the door shut. It bounced back from the caked mud on the threshold, so he kicked it again. He leaned the yoke against the wall near the washstand. "They're pretty good boys, Cissie. Sometimes they have to learn the hard way, but they're pretty good boys."

Casey was not quite in agreement with Pa.

"I couldn't see too good through that window," he said. "What'd you do to old Eldon?"

"I put the stove lifter down his neck."

"The stove lifter?" Pa whacked his leg. "That beats all!" He laughed until tears came to his eyes. "So that's why he jumped around like a turpentined dog."

Casey did not share the humor. "I asked you to talk to them, Mr. Bragg."

Pa waved the idea away. "They don't learn sic-'em by hearing talk. They got to find things out for themselves."

"And you left me alone for them to—to—"

Pa eyed her harshly. "Don't forget, you knew what you was getting into when you came here. I ain't going to be no wet nurse, Cissie. When those boys decide you ain't what they think you are, they'll start behaving. Maybe."

"Do you think Eldon will now?"

"You didn't do nothing but scorch his back. What did that tell him about you?" Pa pointed at Casey with a long finger. "The day Eldon decides you're a decent woman, there won't be nobody dare look sidewise at you when he's around."

"And Harve?"

Pa shook his head. "As far as he knows, the only decent women there is is his ma and sisters. You'll have trouble with Harve."

It was a bleak prospect. Once more Casey told herself she had walked into it knowingly. She did think, however, that Pa Bragg was more on her side than he was letting on.

"You didn't ask about Boston," Pa said. "Why not?"

"Well, he didn't seem very forward. I just—"

"Yeah. Boston has his own ways. It won't be him that's after you. It'll more likely be the other way around."

"No. I didn't come here to find a husband, Mr. Bragg."

"Who said anything about a husband?"

"Or a lover, either."

Pa chuckled. "Now we've covered the whole family, except for me."

"You're a married man, Mr. Bragg."

"You bet. And you think that makes me like the stones of the mountains when it comes to a pretty young woman?"

Casey couldn't tell whether he was trying to scare her or not. "It should," she said hastily. "I've got to do the dishes." She wanted to add that she was very tired. While she went about her chores, her muscles trembled from fatigue. Once more the heat of the room began to get to her.

"You didn't eat," Pa said.

"I didn't feel like it."

"Puny, eh? That's the trouble with most women."

"I am not puny!"

"Hah!" Pa made two trips to the woodpile, and then he put on his sheepskin and took the yoke and the water pails. Grateful for the cold air of the open doorway, Casey watched him crunch his way across the starlit snow. She was feeling better when he returned a few

108

minutes later with the buckets of water. Ice was frozen in streaks on the sides of the pails, and the rims were beaded with it.

"It's going to be a bear cat tonight." Pa sat down and put his hands behind his head.

"Have you made up your mind about my staying here, Mr. Bragg?"

"Nope. If you didn't have a name like Cissie Leclair, it would be some easier to decide, or if you acted like a woman with that sort of name is supposed to act, then it would be simpler, too."

"At least you've decided I'm not a female detective?"

"Nope. I ain't settled my mind on that, either."

In profile, Pa's deep-lined face looked gaunt. The lamplight put a touch of sallowness under the weathering. From the side, the John Brown impression was entirely lost. Casey thought she was beginning to learn something of the character of his sons, but Pa himself would never be easy to understand.

He rose suddenly and took a box of soda from a shelf. "I don't figure how they thought they could flatten me with a couple of drinks. I faked the third one, the same way they was doing. I just don't figure it at all. They know better."

Pa mixed soda and water in a tin cup and drank it with a noisy sound. "I got to admit, though, them drinks turned my belly into a sour pickle vat. Jehoshaphat!" He made a face.

Casey finished her work. "Good night, Mr. Bragg."

"Yeah. Better leave that door open, less'n you want to freeze. Won't do no good to close it, anyway, seeing as there's no bar on it."

Casey knew he was watching her all the way across the room. She closed the door and got into bed as quickly as she could. The blankets and heavy comforters were a cold weight that warmed slowly, and the chill of the hay-stuffed mattress persisted for a long time.

Pa didn't go to bed right away. Casey heard him belching. His boots scraped on the floor, and his chair creaked. Though she finally warmed a limited area of the bed, she still could not sleep. Pa's presence in the other room made her uneasy. After a time she rose quietly and tiptoed to the door and opened it a crack.

Pa was sitting at the table, a fierce frown of concentration on his brow. He was reading the big Bible. Without moving his head, he said, "I told you you ought to leave that door open."

Startled, Casey banged the door shut and scampered back to her bed. Sometime later she was dozing when noise in the other room roused her. Pa was putting wood in the stove. And then he tramped off to bed.

None of the events tightly packed into the previous few days crossed Casey's mind as she began to doze again. She recalled, instead, the day she received the ribbon bookmark for being the best pupil in Sunday school. At fourteen, in the same white-spired church at the crossroads near her father's home, she had taught youngsters their Bible lessons.

She heard her father talking in his soft, humorous way. "Some of the worst fleecings I've taken were from men who quoted the Bible beautifully. The Book hadn't failed, but the men had."

The house creaked as cold settled hard upon it. Dimly through her drowsiness Casey heard Pa snoring. She fell asleep then.

# CHAPTER 10

*"I know all about her being called a Cattle Kate, but I'll stake my life that it was a dirty lie. There never was a finer woman."* Richard O. Gibson, former Cattlemen's Association detective, Tempe, Arizona, 1931.

PA BRAGG WARMED HIS BACK AT THE BUNKHOUSE stove and regarded his battered, arnica-odorous sons with mingled scorn and fondness.

"You going to let her stay?" Harve asked.

"Them was awful fine pancakes this morning, Pa," Eldon said. "Real fine."

"Sure now." Pa nodded.

"Good coffee," Boston said.

Having taken fearful abuse because of the utter failure of his long icicle theory, Pinky thought it wise not to say anything, but he hoped Pa would say he was going to send her away. And yet he didn't want her to go.

Pa let his sons run on for a while, and then he said, "Did it ever occur to you jugheads that she could be a detective?"

"Naw!" Eldon said, and then he blinked and tried to think about it.

Harve shook his head. "They wouldn't send a woman after us."

"Not with you around," Boston said, grinning. His left eye was black and swollen.

"That's about the only thing they ain't sent," Pa said.

Pinky had a bad sinking feeling. She sure had been

friendly with the railroaders. "Railroad detective?" he asked.

"Cattlemen?" Eldon asked.

"That store at Lake City?" Boston looked thoughtful.

"Maybe one of the mines where we got all that—" Harve began.

"That's enough!" Pa growled. "You don't have to go over our whole damn history." He was pretty certain in his own mind that Casey was no detective, but it didn't hurt now and then to try to keep his sons on their toes.

"Maybe we ought to quit stealing—for a few days, or something," Eldon suggested.

"Yeah," Harve said. "What with the snow and cold, it won't hardly pay to go prowling around."

"We could stay right here at home for a spell, couldn't we?" Pa said.

Harve and Eldon said, "Yeah!"

"And that would give you all a chance to hang around the house and cause me no end of trouble, like last night."

"Oh, we wasn't thinking of that," Harve protested.

"Naw," said Eldon. "Gosh, no."

Pa sighed. "It's a scandal the way you boys bamboozle your poor old pa." He went to the window and scraped a place to see through. "We got work to do. You've been loafing around here like some nabob's sons all during the storm, living on the fat of the land, the way that Cissie girl cooks."

"I wasn't loafing, Pa," Pinky said.

"Oh, no! No, Pinky, you was gallivanting around the country, making big deals for cooks and things, bringing home five-dollar horses and jugs of whiskey, most of it inside you."

The laughter struck, and Pinky wished he'd learn to

112

keep his mouth shut.

"It's Christmas, Pa," Eldon said. "We ought to take a little rest on Christmas."

"I was figuring on cutting a tree and taking it over to the house, and then we could play some music and sort of have a time." Harve looked at his brothers, urging them to support his sudden idea.

"That does sound interesting," Boston said.

"It sure does," Pa said. "Four of you over there fiddling around with a tree for two minutes and then figuring to fiddle around with Cissie the rest of the time. Nope, I've got worries enough. You're going to take them six steers out there up to Old Camp, along with that beautiful, wonderful racehorse Pinky brought in, and then you're going to butcher them and store them in the snow just like the others we got here and there."

"Why can't we butcher them right here?" Harve asked.

"Sure, sure, and have some snooper ride in right in the middle of things. You know better than that, Harve."

"We'll leave a big trail to Old Camp," Eldon said.

Pa shook his head. He was running out of patience. "Not the way the wind's coming up. No more argufying. I've said what you're going to do."

The boys looked at each other. It was settled.

"How soon?" Harve sighed. Him out in the cold snow, when he could just as well be in the house making hay with Casey. If Eldon hadn't shoved in last night and ruined everything with his dumb strong-arm method . . .

"Right now!" Pa said.

"Not even Christmas dinner?" Pinky mourned.

"Folks like us who sit around eating a big Christmas dinner, with six of Ross Chamberlain's steers in the

113

corral, stand the best chance of all of getting caught with our pants down," Pa declared. "Not that I don't favor Christmas."

"With the snow and the butchering and all, it'll be an overnight trip," Harve said, glancing at his brothers.

"You're plumb right," Pa said cheerfully. He went out, took a deep breath, and bellowed, "Get around!" His roar rolled out across the deep, sparkling snow where gusts of light wind were scudding the fluff like white dust. The geese made a racket, as if seconding the command.

In the house, Casey went to the door with a dishrag in her hand to see what the yell was all about. Pa was striding toward the barn, with the dogs Thum and Cougar at his heels.

It was a beautifully clear day with the sun above distant snowy mountains. Casey stepped out for a better look. In the meadow below the corrals the snow was swirling around a mower that looked so stark and lonely that it seemed it must be feeling the cold. Beyond the meadow the hill rose gently to an aspen ridge where the tree trunks a quarter of a mile, the wind was tossing spumes of snow like smoke.

Casey soon knew there was no heat in the sun, though it threw a smashing reflection off the snow that made her eyes water as she squinted at the scene. Her footsteps squeaked as she hurried inside, and the dishrag in her hand froze stiff.

The conductor on the train had told her that it sometimes was so cold that smoke from the engines froze in solid chunks before it could dissipate, and then in warmer weather fell in fluffy masses on the track and had to be shoveled off.

She was about ready to believe the story.

Pa's boys were stirring around in the bunkhouse. When he yelled, it meant business. They put on heavy clothing and blackened the area around their eyes with charcoal to ward off snow blindness from the glare, and were generally uncheerful.

"At least I got only one eye to fix," Boston said. "Was that your elbow, Harve?"

"I hope so. I'm damn sure you're the one that cracked my ribs with that piece of chair. I sure ain't in very good shape to be riding."

"Tell that to Pa," Eldon said. "Then he'll let you stay here with him and Casey. Haw!"

"You know what he's up to, don't you?" Harve asked. "Getting us away overnight. That ain't hard to figure out."

"Pa—him?" Eldon couldn't believe it.

"Yeah, him! You think he's a hundred years old? Don't be simple. We're going up to Old Camp to freeze our asses off, and he's staying here to have a gay old time with Casey." Harve snorted. "He's had that in mind ever since he seen her. Why do you think he came busting in last night, whaling us with that yoke? He's jealous, that's why."

"From where I sat, I didn't see nobody get far enough to cause any jealousy," Boston said, "especially old Chief Hot Shirt there."

"I should have busted your head last night," Eldon growled. He put his skullcap on over his thick, spiky hair. "Come to think on it, that's exactly what Pa's up to. Do you reckon he'll do any good for himself?"

"You just bet on it," Harve said. "He's sneaky. He won't be near as clumsy-footed as us. The whole house full and us trying to get at her . . . Why, no woman but some drunken old hag would take that kind of thing. It just wasn't a good idea."

"You thought it up," Boston said.

"I don't care who thought it up! It was a bum stunt."

"It sure was." Boston grinned. He put a sweater on over his two shirts.

"Someday we got to take a stand against the way Pa chouses us around," Harve declared. He suffered for a while with his thoughts of what was going to happen to Casey while they were gone. "I can just see him when we come dragging in half froze. He'll have a big sneaky smile on his face, and he'll say, 'Boys, I've decided to let her stay.' "

Eldon stopped moving, with one arm already in his sheepskin. "It don't hardly seem right."

"You're all wrong," Pinky said suddenly. "If he was after her, he wouldn't have to chase us away. Hell, he stays in the house at night, and we're over here."

That gave them pause for a time. Then Harve said, "It's the idea of having us around when he's doing something like that. It makes him nervous."

"I'd be nervous, too, if somebody was prowling around the house three, four times on a cold night while I was trying to get a little," Boston said. "Which I don't say Pa was."

"Only twice!" Harve said. "I had to get up anyway, so I just strolled over that way."

"The hell!" Eldon's big eyes popped eagerly. "What was going on?"

"Nothing," Harve admitted.

"See there!" Pinky said. "I hope you froze your butt."

They had stalled about as long as they could. Boston checked the heater. The fire was almost out. Eldon stood glumly with one hand on the door latch. "It ain't

116

right. What are we going to do about it?"

"We go up to Old Camp and freeze our asses off," Boston answered.

They did not love him for his answer, but they realized he had spoken truly of their unhappy lot, and so they went forth into the rising wind and blustering cold. "Brass monkeys, that's what we're going to be," Harve grumped, looking toward the house.

The greatest shock was yet ahead.

Pa's horse was saddled, and he was waiting for them.

"You—you going a ways with us, Pa?" Harve asked.

"What do you mean—a ways?"

"Well, I thought—we thought—that is—"

"Stop mumbling," Pa said. "You thought I was trying to pull something, didn't you?"

The Bragg boys looked at each other like children caught with their thoughts, if not their paws, in the cookie jar.

"Saddle up," Pa ordered. His face was stern. He didn't grin until he turned away from his sons to fiddle with his cinch.

Harve moved with great difficulty. He kept touching his ribs, and his face was a study in pain. "I'm afraid my busted ribs are sticking into my lungs," he said at last, after Pa paid no attention to his dedication to duty under extreme travail.

"That'll help ventilate 'em," Pa said. "I had one whole side of ribs shot loose at Pea Ridge. You could see my lungs heaving like a bunch of hot guts in a sack, but I kept on shooting my rifle for an hour, and then I walked a half mile to an ambulance wagon."

Harve forgot his ribs, but a little later he put his arms across his stomach, doubled over, and moaned.

"Belly trouble now?" Pa asked.

117

"Awful." Harve's expression would have wrung compassion from a grindstone. "You know how a bad belly feels."

"Yes, I do, Harve boy." Pa nodded sympathetically.

It was just a matter of the proper ailment, Harve thought. "It must have been that whiskey last night. I think I froze my guts."

"Well, now . . ." Pa was real concerned.

"Maybe if somebody could help me back to the bunkhouse . . ." Harve groaned in agony. "It hit me in the night. I didn't hardly sleep a wink."

"That must be a fact," Pa said. "I heard you tramping around the house half the night. Now finish saddling that horse. Since your guts are froze up anyway, the ride can't make 'em no worse."

Casey opened the door to throw out the debris she had scraped from the floor with a shovel. She heard the burst of laughter at the barn and wondered what so amused the Braggs. They rode away shortly afterward, driving six steers. Pinky was trailing, with his stolen sorrel on a lead rope. The steers kept trying to break back to the corral. Thum and Cougar tried eagerly to help the riders, but the snow was too much for the dogs. Pa sent them back to the house with a yell, where they sat in the yard, whining and trembling.

They could ride, those Braggs, Casey had to allow. Even the monstrous Eldon, on a heavy chestnut, was a rider to admire. Boston, she thought, was the best of all; he rode with an economy of motion, with a flowing skill that appeared almost effortless, though his horse was kicking up clouds of snow and lunging unevenly as it helped line out the reluctant steers.

It was a scramble for a while, but the Braggs got the

118

steers into single file and headed up the valley, into the teeth of the piercing wind that was making a choppy white sea of the meadow. The bawling protests began to fade away. Casey went back to work.

The time on the clock she had set by guess that morning was eight o'clock. Eight in the morning on Christmas Day in the year of 1886, at an all-male ranch somewhere in the frozen Rockies. She, Casey Leclair.

For a few moments she lingered on her real name, on memories of Christmases at home. She wondered what her family was doing at this very moment.

It was too much remembering.

She dipped her mop into the bucket of lye water and resumed scrubbing. She had to go now from where she was each day; wallowing in memories was no good.

Someday . . . Someday, perhaps, she would go home for a visit.

It was six hours later before she made a pot of gunpowder tea and sat down to rest. The floor was twice scrubbed then, the brown wetness of it just beginning to dry to the color of the lye she had used in the wooden bucket. She had cleaned and dusted the whole room, hanging stray clothing and gear on nails on the end wall near Pa's room. She had emptied the overflowing ash pan, burned the litter of trash in the bottom of the woodbox, and filled the woodbox from the huge pile outside.

All the caked grease was gone from the stove, and now it looked much better in its smug coat of dull black polish. Bread dough was rising on the warming oven, and a big roast was almost done. The wash boiler was thumping on the stove, and a tub she had stumbled over in the snow while shoveling a path to the woodpile was sitting on the floor. In a few minutes she was going to bathe and then wash her clothes. She had strung a rope near the stove to dry them.

She opened the door to let some of the steamy vapor out. When she closed it a few minutes later, she almost fell on the icy surface that had formed on the damp floor near the door.

How long did the infernal cold last?

The geese honked their warning while she was bathing. Then Thum and Cougar raised muffled barks from their dugout kennel in the hill. A few moments later they were in the yard, making their deep-chested sounds.

A man hailed the house.

"Just a minute!" Casey yelled. Then she remembered that the door was unbarred. "Stay out!"

The tubby little man was standing by his horse when Casey got around to opening the door. Apparently he was known around the place, for the dogs had barked at him only a short time. He showed no surprise on seeing Casey. "They ain't here, huh?"

"No."

The man's face was dark with cold. Ice was hanging at the corners of his ragged, bushy mustache. He was jigging up and down as he held his arms across his chest, and his breath was making vapor squirrel tails.

"Come in," Casey said.

He was quick to accept the invitation, but still he paused to wipe his feet on the gunnysacks Casey had spread on the wide step at the doorway. He dropped his gloves on the woodbox and scrubbed his hands above the stove. "It's getting colder every winter, I swear." He peered at Casey over his shoulder, an inoffensive-looking man whose mild round eyes gave the impression of having asked questions that no one could answer since the day he was born. "So you're Miss Leclair?"

"How did you know?"

"I just came up from Sapinero." The man seemed to think that was sufficient explanation.

"Where's that?"

"Down there—on the railroad. You know."

Oh, yes, the blessed railroad. No doubt by now talk of her arrival in Cimarron and departure with Pinky Bragg had been carried from one end of the line to the other.

"I'm Caleb Penfield," the man said. "My place is over there." He pointed vaguely. "Most folks just call me Onreliable."

"Onreliable?" The pronunciation confused Casey.

"Because I lie quite a bit, I suppose, but only about things that don't matter." His eyes took in the room. He caught sight of the tub Casey had dragged against the wall near the stove and walked over to look at it. She had thrown her soiled clothes into it. "Washing in this weather?"

"Yes."

"Ain't it a chore, though?" Onreliable went back to the stove. Something in his pockets clinked as he unbuttoned his mackinaw coat and waved the bottom of it toward the heat. He reminded Casey of a little bird fluffing its feathers in a dust bath. "Busting through the snow from Sap was quite a chore, too."

"Would you like something to eat?"

Onreliable nodded. "I'd be obliged." He took off his coat and hung it on a chair. "Where'd you say they went?"

"I didn't say."

"Where did they go?"

"I don't know, Mr. Penfield."

"You really don't?"

"No. Tell me, how did you get here so quickly after the geese first honked?"

"Oh, I didn't come up the meadow road. I just sort of popped over the hill." Onreliable eyed the tub of water. "It's all right to tell me where they went. I'm their friend."

"That's nice. If you'll sit there at the table, I'll fix you something to eat. I won't have any bread because I'm just getting ready to bake, but if you can get along with crackers—"

"I eat lots of crackers. They're fine."

Sitting at the table, Onreliable wrinkled his pudgy nose when Casey took the beef roast from the oven. "Oh, my gosh, would you look at that!"

"Will tea be all right, Mr. Penfield?"

"Gosh, yes!"

His questioning eyes followed Casey's every move. Even as he ate with an appetite astonishing for one of his size, he watched her. He drank four cups of tea and sucked his mustache gently. "I wouldn't let him see in that pantry."

"Who?"

"Tricky Dick."

"You'll have to speak more clearly, Mr. Penfield. I've been here only a short time."

"That's hard for me to do, being so used to lying for the fun of it. People get mad at me sometimes, I know, but—"

"Who is Tricky Dick?"

"Gibson. Dick Gibson. He says he's a trapper, but I know better. He's a detective for the cowmen." Onreliable studied Casey's breasts. He pushed at his mustache with one finger.

122

"Go on."

"He come in last night, in a boxcar with two horses. Oh, he's got a trapping outfit all right, but first he's going to scout around looking for a place to trap. He says." Onreliable blinked. "Say, you ain't got much on under that dress, have you?"

Casey picked up the dishes. "Since you've finished your meal, Mr. Penfield, I strongly suggest that you—"

"Wait a minute!" Onreliable raised his hand. "Joel Bragg wouldn't like for me to leave without saying what I come here to tell him through all that snow and ferocious cold, even if he ain't here."

"Then get to the point or get out."

"Whew! You don't beat around the bush, do you?"

"I recommend the same procedure to you, Mr. Penfield."

Onreliable nodded admiringly. "I wish I could use words like that." He preened his mustache. It fell back over his lip in a ragged drape as soon as his finger left it. "Now where was we? Oh, yeah, Tricky Dick Gibson. We had a big poker game going most all night in the section house. He got right in the middle of it, asking cute little questions now and then. I played real dumb . . ."

Casey decided that Onreliable never had and never would talk tersely, so she let him run on. The meat of his rambling was that Gibson, whom he had smelled out as a cattlemen's detective, though Onreliable did not explain precisely how he had done so, was undoubtedly at the moment on his way to the Bragg ranch, expecting to find stolen steers. At great risk and personal sacrifice of comfort because he was a devoted friend of Joel Bragg, Onreliable had come to warn him.

"There are no cattle here that I know of," Casey said.

"I know. I seen the tracks going up toward Old Camp.

The way she's blowing, they won't be there much longer. To tell the truth, even as careful as Joel is, I didn't figure him to go out on a day like this, so I thought—"

"I'm sure he'll appreciate it. I'll tell him when he comes back." Casey paused. "I assume you stay in the bunkhouse when you're here?"

"Oh, I'm not staying today. I don't want Tricky Dick to find me here. No, sir!" Onreliable didn't move. "I was lucky in the poker game last night, Miss Leclair."

"Congratulations. I have a lot of work to do yet, so—"

"I know, I know, but I'd have to build a fire if I went over to the bunkhouse." Onreliable lifted his arms as Casey washed the table, and then he put them down again. "Them railroaders are fierce to gossip."

"No doubt."

"I was real lucky in that game." Onreliable clinked heavy silver in his pocket. The innocence of his look had now turned to slyness.

The miserable little wretch, Casey thought. But it was to be expected.

Onreliable stacked five silver dollars on the table.

"I thought you said you were very lucky in the game, Mr. Penfield."

Onreliable's face brightened, and then cupidity threw a quick shadow across his eagerness. "Maybe I lied about that. You know how I am."

Casey had her moves planned now. She began to gather the lamps from the wall brackets. "I don't think these wicks have been trimmed or the chimneys washed since Mr. Bragg left."

Onreliable added five dollars to the stack. He riffled the coins slowly, one by one. "That's a pretty fair price, I'd say."

Casey went on with her work. "Is it, Mr. Penfield?"

Onreliable watched her brightly. He added three dollars to the stack. "Oh my, that's an unlucky number." He took one away. "That's all the money I got in the world."

"You had one more on there a second ago."

"But it made thirteen! That's unlucky."

"Try fifteen."

Onreliable added the three dollars. Casey picked the money up. The little man rose briskly. "I knew we could get along," he said, putting his arm around Casey.

"Your pockets are still rattling, Mr. Penfield."

"We already made the deal."

Casey sighed. "I suppose so." They took a few steps toward her bedroom. She stopped and put both hands on Onreliable's shoulders. "There's just one thing."

"No more money! We agreed."

He was in perfect position then. Casey shoved him hard in the shoulders. He went back two steps, his legs hit the edge of the tub, and he sat down with a mighty splash.

He did not try to rise, but sat there jackknifed into the tub, with his hands on the rim. "It wasn't enough, huh?" he asked sadly.

Casey gathered up the silver dollars that he had scattered across the floor and threw them into his lap. "Now get out of here!"

Onreliable studied her face with keen interest. "I'll go another ten dollars."

"Get out!"

"I'm sorry for being a cheapskate. Thirty-five dollars."

On pegs above the clock shelf was a flintlock rifle that Casey had dusted that morning. She knew very little of firearms, though enough to hold the piece and point the right end at Onreliable's middle.

"That won't shoot a lick. It ain't primed or nothing. But never mind, I'm beginning to see the light." Onreliable heaved himself out of the tub, and then he turned and began to fish around in the water for silver dollars that had fallen off his lap. A pair of Casey's lace-trimmed drawers were draped across his backside.

Casey had to resist the urge to laugh.

The drawers fell as Onreliable was stooped over, dabbling in the tub. He reached back through his legs and put them into the water. "Oh, my." He found his money and turned to face Casey. "I'm fearful wet. I'll have to stay and—"

Casey opened the door. "Get out, I said." His horse, she observed, had wandered out of the biting wind and was at the barn.

Onreliable picked up his belongings and waddled toward the bunkhouse like a child who has wet its pants. Casey had barely closed the door, it seemed, when he returned, calling out piteously. "It's freezing over there. Look!" He held up his hands to show his frozen sleeves. When he moved, his pants crackled with ice.

"Build a fire." Casey shut the door.

While she was mopping up, she found a silver dollar leaning on its edge against the bottom of the range. She put it on the washstand near the door.

Onreliable returned sometime later, wearing dry pants that were rolled up at the bottoms. "I'm short a dollar."

Casey tossed it to him.

"Was it me or too low a price?"

"It was me!" Casey said. "Someone lied to you."

Onreliable began to shiver. "Joel Bragg ain't going to like this, after me risking my very life in the snow, coming here to—"

"Shall I tell him everything, Mr. Penfield?"

Onreliable thought a moment. "I guess not."

"Good day." Casey shut the door. It closed easily now that the mud was off the threshold.

From the window she watched Onreliable trot to the barn. He did not ride directly up the valley, but went across the meadow, where snowy gusts twice engulfed him. The end of his horse's tail was streaming downwind.

Casey felt a little sorry for him, but more sympathetic toward the animal.

By the time the bread was baked, Casey had four dried apple pies ready for the oven. Four pies might last one meal, the way the Braggs ate. She gathered Pa's dirty clothes from his room and put them in the boiler. After the pies were baked, she cut two pieces of beef and called the dogs. They caught the meat in the air and gobbled it down without letting it touch the snow. They would not come near the door, and they backed away cautiously when Casey tried to go to them.

Later they followed her down to the barn. That was another place they had been trained not to enter, for they sat down outside when she opened the door. It seemed warm inside. Casey saw a little buckskin horse and two tall-shouldered blue mules in the stalls. In a tight storeroom she saw saddles neatly treed and well-oiled harness hanging on pegs. A tin-lined oat bin was almost full. The shelves were stocked with greases and salves. There were sacks of grain and cracked corn, one of the latter open, with a two-pound lard bucket in it.

It was a rat-proof storeroom, in much better order than she had found the house.

She dipped corn into the lard bucket and went out the

127

side door. From the edge of an unfrozen pond a gander rushed at her, beating his wings. Five other geese came from a low log structure and added to the gabbling. The gander stopped a few feet from her, craning his neck, his eyes bright and beady, but he did not join the other geese when she scattered the cracked corn.

The dogs, canny Thum and Cougar, peered from around the corner of the barn.

Vapor was rising from the pond and along a small flow that supplied the pool from the spring not far above it. Below the pond was a mass of ice, and there was no evidence of water flow farther down the meadow.

Except for one blind spot where the barn blocked a view of the hill behind the house, the site was admirably situated for the geese to see a long way in all directions.

It was too cold to linger. Casey turned to go. The gander came up behind her in a silent charge and rapped her twice on the leg. Even through her heavy skirts it was enough to make her gasp with pain. "Why, you treacherous old devil!" she cried.

The gander closed his wings and began to eat cracked corn with the other geese.

Hurrying back to the house through the biting wind, Casey stopped long enough to get an armful of wood. She was shivering when she got inside. It was much colder, she was sure, than at any time during her trip with Pinky. Any detective who would ride in weather like this in a forlorn effort to surprise the Braggs was either stupid or very determined.

Not long afterward Casey had a chance to decide which, for the man did come.

Her washing was draped on chairs and on the line near the stove when she heard the geese give the warning. Then the dogs barked. This time she was able to look down-valley because she had washed the four-paned window in the end wall of the house.

He came against the wind, on a big sorrel that left white streamers fleeing from its hoofs, riding unbent before the gusts, conveying a sharp attitude of alertness, though he was still a long distance away. There was no hesitation in his manner, but Casey saw him moving his head as he studied the buildings, and when he was a hundred yards away, she saw him slip his right hand from its glove.

The dogs growled and barked and circled his horse when he rode into the yard. They accepted Casey's authority when she told them to be quiet.

"Are you alone here?" His deep-set eyes were dark, and his face was dark with a two-day growth of beard.

"Yes." He was about thirty-five, Casey guessed. Wind swirled around the corner of the house, driving fine, dry snow against his clothing. "Won't you come in?" Casey almost added his name.

"Thanks. First I'll get my horse out of this." He rode toward the barn. He was there for at least ten minutes before Casey saw him walking back, a tall, long-striding man with grace in his movements.

He looked at all the inside doorways quickly when he came into the room. There was a restless, listening attitude about him; he seemed to be a man who was always looking beyond what was immediately before him. Casey had known gamblers like that, men who were always trying to reach a fraction ahead of now.

Seeing him at close range, Casey revised her estimate of his age; he was closer to twenty-five than thirty-five. "My name is Gibson," he said.

He must be thoroughly chilled, Casey thought, but he had not rushed to the stove to rub his hands, which seemed to be a habit of Western men. "What is your business here?" she asked.

"Do I have to have business?"

"I certainly would think so, to travel on a day like this."

Gibson nodded. He took off his heavy coat. He was wearing a pistol shoved under his belt on the left side. "Somebody came in just ahead of me."

Casey said nothing.

"Who was it, Miss Leclair?"

"Another trapper."

Gibson's attitude was sharp, unsmiling. "It was that little windbag Penfield."

Casey watched him quietly. "Would you like something to eat?"

"Thank you, yes. It smells wonderful in here. In fact, it's the first clean place I've seen in a long time."

Casey studied him while he was eating. His manners were good. He ate with a hearty appetite, unhurriedly, yet he gave the impression of having his mind on other business. It was that detachment that took much from his appearance, Casey thought. He was a handsome man in poise and physical equipment, but his face was too still, lacking the brightness of mobility. He was weighing something, waiting.

It was not just the present situation that made him that way, Casey sensed; it was his nature.

"Are you the Braggs' fancy woman, Miss Leclair?" he asked suddenly.

The question took Casey by surprise. She waited a moment to gain her balance and to calm her quick anger. "News seems to travel quickly."

"It's a thinly settled country. We don't have too much to talk about." Gibson paused. "Is it true?" There was an odd, compelling quietness in his tone, as if he had to have an honest answer but had no personal interest in it. Casey felt that he would react exactly the same if she said yes or no.

And that enraged her. "If it's any of your business, Mr. Gibson, I'm the cook here, and that's all!"

He studied her, mulling over the answer. "You're a good one. I hope the Braggs appreciate you."

She decided he was the most irritating man she had ever met.

"Where are they today?"

"I have no idea!"

"Not even the direction they went, or when?"

The tracks had been almost leveled out when Casey went down to feed the geese. Perhaps they had been entirely lost when Gibson came. She glanced toward the window, but it was frosted over again. "Help yourself to more beef, Mr. Gibson."

"Thank you."

Casey filled his coffee cup.

"You're using a better brand of coffee than I'm used to." Gibson looked at the storeroom door.

While confusion and a touch of worry still lay on Casey's face, Gibson said casually, "What do you owe the Braggs?"

"I work here!" Casey wished she could be calm; generally she had very good control of her responses.

"That's a good answer," Gibson said. "You know who I am, of course."

"Do I?"

"Why, yes." Gibson looked at her seriously. "But if Penfield hadn't told you, I think you would have figured it out, anyway. Besides being very attractive, you're intelligent."

He meant it, Casey knew, but he said it like a statement of fact, instead of a compliment. Damn such a cold fish!

He finished his meal and sat looking at her, and then she saw the rising interest in his expression, the drive that was seldom far below the surface in all males. Every man who had heard of her believed that his battle was half won already because of what he had heard; the rest was merely opportunity, or, as in Onreliable's case, a matter of price.

"You rode in here openly with the intention of catching the Braggs with—in—some violation of law, I suppose. There are five of them, on their own home ground. What kind of man are you, Mr. Gibson?"

"The violation you stammered over was a matter of eight steers belonging to—Stolen steers, Miss Leclair, which were driven away from here just this morning."

"And there were five men."

Gibson shook his head. "They're not killers."

"But you are?"

Gibson's eyes were quiet and bitter—and old. "I did not come here to kill anyone."

But he would kill if he had to. Casey took it no further; she had ripped through his armor, and there was no need to punish him more. He must be a very lonely man—and then she wondered if that was just her idea. It was too easy—and dangerous—to try to understand people in terms of one's own feelings.

Gibson went to the window and scratched a hole in the frost. "The marks you were wondering about a minute ago are still there—just barely."

"They won't be for long. They'll disappear by the time you've ridden a mile." Casey set a stove lid aside to put wood in the stove. They reached for a stick at the

132

same time, and Gibson's hand came down on top of hers.

If he had been rough and demanding, she would have reacted against him instantly, but there was a soothing gentleness in the way he moved to take her in his arms. She was there suddenly, not quite understanding how it had happened. It was bewildering, for nothing like that had happened to her since she first knew Billy Carpenter.

He kissed her gently at first and then with increasing, demanding pressure, and then she was no longer disarmed by his quiet approach; it was only part of his cold-blooded, calculating nature. She pushed away from him so violently that she would have staggered backward across the room if he had not caught her wrists.

"I don't know whether to let you go or not, young lady."

She tried to jerk loose. "Are you sure?" he asked.

"Let go of me!"

His look was cool and appraising. "Are you afraid of me or yourself?"

"I'm sick of every man I've met lately!"

"Oh? Lately," he mused. He let her go then.

She grabbed her snow-dipping pot from the top of the warming oven and scooped it partly full of scalding water in the boiler.

"Pour it back," Gibson said. "You've made your point."

His lack of fear was infuriating. Casey's arm was drawn back, ready to deliver the hot water. She had a good notion to throw it, anyway.

Gibson turned his back on her and picked up his hat and coat. "By the way, your washing will freeze dry if you hang it outside. All you have to do is shake the frost out of it."

"Thank you for your kind advice!" There she was doing it again, speaking in anger when there was no need.

"And thank you for the meal." Gibson paused at the door. He smiled then for the first time. It was a bleak expression, rueful, but it changed his character for an instant, breaking the still tenseness of his expression. "We both have a hard row to hoe, Miss Leclair."

And then he was gone.

Casey watched him go down to the corrals and on to the barn. He rode up the valley, into the scudding clouds of powder snow. There wasn't enough daylight left for him to get very far that afternoon, even if the trail remained.

She saw horse and rider suddenly enveloped in rolling white fog that broke in streamers around them. Up there the valley narrowed and the trees came down and the snow would be deeper. He would have to camp out in that awful cold, with loneliness gnawing at his soul.

A hard row to hoe . . .

Yes, they were alike, and if he had chosen to stay . . .

Casey was glad that he had gone on.

# CHAPTER 11

*"Until the day he died, sometime before 1890, my Uncle Ross swore that she was a robbers'-roost whore who never did a lick of work and sat around all decked out in finery, with the Braggs waiting on her hand and foot. I don't know. I saw her only*

134

*once. She did have on a fancy dress, and her hair was real short, but maybe it was just growing back after typhoid. My impression was that she was a beautiful woman. I was just a boy then."* Kevin B. Chamberlain, theater manager, Baltimore, Maryland, 1929.

WIND, A HOWLING MONSTER WITH A BANSHEE VOICE, woke Casey in the dead of night. She was huddled under heavy covers with only her nose exposed, and she was shivering. Though her door had been open all day and she had left a fire in the kitchen on retiring, the place was like an icebox.

She got up and lit her lamp. The flame wavered in a frigid draft. While she was getting more quilts from the trunk, she saw the tweed wall drapery billowing like curtains at an open window. She added the covers to the bed, then dove back into it so quickly that she forgot to blow out the lamp. The quilts did not help; they were only more weight compressing her deeper into a puddle of cold.

She gave up trying to sleep and went out to replenish the fire. It had burned out. Crosscurrents of icy air were coursing through the room. A pan of water she had left on the stove was frozen. The heavy cast-iron teakettle was intact only because it had boiled dry before the fire went out. Before retiring she had shifted her clothesline from the area of the stove to the corner of the room near Pa's bedroom.

She could tell by the way the clothes were swaying gently in the draft that they were frozen stiff.

The kindled fire was slow in taking hold. She kept lifting the lid to see how it was doing. At last it caught, and then she filled the firebox with wood. The top of the

135

stove was beginning to throw heat when the wind changed. Puffs of smoke sprang from around the lids, and then smoke began to roll out of every seam. The room was soon choking full of it as it poured even from the ash door which she had opened for better draft.

If she had one real fear, it was of fire. Her father's barn had burned one night, and they had not gotten the horses out.

She opened the door. A numbing blast of wind threw particles of ice against her nightgown, and the smoke came from the stove worse than ever. She closed the door and ran back to her room, dressing as quickly as she could. Smoke, she tried to reason, could not burn the house down, but she was too shaken to analyze the mechanics of the stove. It was not working properly, so it might cause something to catch fire.

She ran back to the smoke-filled kitchen, grabbed the wash boiler, and went outside. When she hit the hard-packed snow at the bottom of the step, she went sprawling, hurling the boiler ahead of her. Lying there in the pale starlight with the breath knocked out of her, she saw the wind catch the boiler and skate it across the riffled surface of the snow until it tilted and stopped against a drift.

She rose and stumbled over to it and scooped the boiler through the snow to fill it as best she could. Her skirts were whipping against her legs as she started through the doorway, and then a sudden draft sucked the door shut. It struck the boiler and knocked Casey off the step, back into the yard, spilling the snow on top of her.

As she lay there half stunned for a few moments, with the wind tearing the breath from her mouth, a gust of acrid smoke whipped across her face and she thought the house must be on fire. Doggedly she rose and got more snow, aware that her fingers could barely grasp the handles of the boiler.

The door was jammed. She had to put the boiler down and put her shoulder against the door with all her strength to force it open. Quickly then, gasping from her exertion in the freezing wind, she dragged the boiler inside. The smoke choked her so badly that she had to kneel on the floor until she could clear her lungs.

So set was she on putting out the fire that she took a lid from the stove and was ready to throw snow before she realized the stove was drawing furiously, no longer smoking.

She watched it apprehensively, standing with a double handful of powdery snow. The wind had changed again, she thought. She dumped the snow back into the boiler and held her hands over the stove. After a time the worst of the smoke rolled out, and she shut the door. There was agony in her fingers then, and her eyes were burning, streaming with tears.

And then she saw that the stovepipe was glowing red for half the distance of its short run to the roof, an evil, threatening color that crept higher as she watched. For a while she was close to panic, wanting to dump the boiler full of snow into the fire, to throw snow at the red-hot pipe, but she remembered horrifying stories of steamboats that had blown up from sudden generation of too much steam.

She waited it out. Depending on the wind, the redness of the pipe went up or down, and then it all faded back to black as the wood in the firebox burned down. For the next three hours Casey tended the stove anxiously, learning to judge the amount of fuel she could put in to keep the pipe from growing red clear to the pole roof.

The temperature of the room went up a little, but the

only livable spot was right against the stove, and there she stayed, sitting on a chair with her feet in the oven, watching the pipe, listening to the howling wind, feeding the fire only what she thought was a safe amount of fuel.

It was three-thirty when the wind began to abate. Occasionally strong gusts still made the house shudder, but the swirling fury of it was gone. Now Casey fed the fire all the wood it would take. The room began to warm.

She did not go back to bed. If this was the way it was going to be every time the wind blew, that accursed stove would be a greater problem than the Braggs. Or their visitors.

Where was Gibson now? There had been only a light pack behind his saddle, but surely, like Pinky, he must have known of a cabin somewhere.

She did not worry a moment about the Braggs. They would thrive in any kind of weather, anywhere.

She put the last stick of wood in the fire and fell asleep in the chair. It was after seven when she woke with a guilty start, looking first directly at the pipe. The fire had been out for some time, but she was not cold. Bundling up, she went for wood. The trails she had shoveled the day before to the woodpile and to the out-house were no longer there.

Everywhere the surface of the snow was different. The meadow was no longer a choppy sea, but a quieter run of long swells and curving waves for as far as she could see. Against one side of the barn and other outbuildings the snow was swooped upward in graceful curvature, feathery and bright.

The geese were calling for their breakfast. Thum and Cougar came lunging through the powdery snow. They allowed Casey to pat them on the head, and then they backed off quickly and went somewhere on business of their own.

Though it was still bitter cold, there was a promise of a fair day. And she had work to keep her going.

After breakfast she took Gibson's advice about drying clothes. Pa's things had thawed after the house warmed up, but they were still wet. She hung them outside, where they froze as fast as she put them on the line. Her fingers ached terribly. All her life she was to suffer pain in her joints from extreme cold.

When she shook the clothing an hour later, she saw flakes of frost fly from it, and she found it dry enough to fold and put away in Pa's room.

She did not know how long the Braggs would be away, but bread would keep, so she set a fresh batch of dough, and then she went down to feed the geese, accompanied by the dogs, who once more prudently watched the operation from the corner of the barn. The gander put on his fierce demonstration, but this time Casey did not turn her back on him.

Throwing hay down from the loft for the mules and the little buckskin brought sharp remembrance of the old barn at home. One of her father's big workhorses that she had raised from a colt was named Casey, and that was how she had chosen her first name before going to Miss Leduc's house. The rest had come from a French history book at the Desbien mansion.

Casey. He had been a huge, gentle horse, one of the animals lost when the barn burned.

On the way back to the house she observed that one of the guy wires on the tall pipe was drooping, and that the pipe was leaning badly. That could be the reason for some of her troubles the night before. Access to the roof from the backside of the house was easy. She straightened the pipe and retied the loose guy wire.

As soon as she went inside, she discovered that her tramping about on the roof had caused bits of dirt to fall all over the table, the stove, and the floor. If the rising dough had not been covered with a cloth, it would have been a mess, too.

There would never be an end to work. She was grateful for that. She hoped the Braggs would stay away for a week, or longer.

The sentinel geese raised their furor shortly after two o'clock that afternoon.

Casey saw the riders coming down the valley, Pa in the lead. They were almost at the corrals before she saw that Pinky's horse, trailing as usual, was carrying double.

Gibson was riding behind the saddle.

Pa left his horse for the boys to care for and came on up to the house. He grunted when he saw the gunnysacks that Casey had retrieved that morning from the snowdrift near the bunkhouse. He stomped his feet a time or two and then came in, squinting as his eyes adjusted.

"Feed the geese?" he asked.

"Yes."

"The mules and the horse?"

"Yes."

"What about the dogs?"

"I gave them some meat last night."

Pa grunted. "All right, as long as you don't try to make pets of them. Understand?"

"I understand, Mr. Bragg."

Pa scowled. "What made you so agreeable all of a

140

sudden?" He took off his hat and sheepskin. For a moment Casey thought he was going to throw them on the table, but then he crossed the room and hung them on pegs. "It's awful the way a man gets choused around by some slip of a gal who don't weigh more'n a hundred and twenty pounds dripping wet."

"This is your house. Do as you please."

"You don't have to tell me!" Pa looked at her suspiciously. He made a tour around the place, saying nothing when he saw his freshly washed clothes. He stood in the doorway of Casey's room for a moment. "I supposed you'd have that looking glass hung up by now, considering the great store you seem to set by it."

Casey had put the mirror behind the trunk, glass side to the wall, and there it was going to stay, perhaps for as long as she was at the Bragg ranch.

Pa stopped to look at the bread and pies. He sniffed. "That stuff fit to eat?"

"Oh, I think so. My first five husbands liked it."

"No need for you to tell me how they come to leave you." Pa sat down at the table. "You had things so scrubbed up they was afraid to come in the house." He stretched his legs. "That wind last night like to blowed us out of the shack at Old Camp."

"I imagine. It blew a little here, too."

"Stove smoke?"

"A little."

Pa yawned. "Yeah. She used to complain about that. Ain't nothing to do about it but throw on a little coal oil so she can get to roaring up the pipe good." He rubbed his chin. "Soon's I shave, we'll eat. We got company, I guess you seen."

Casey began to set the table. She had another beef roast in the oven, and potato hash made from what

141

Onreliable and Gibson had left of the first roast. "Yes, I saw him."

"What did you make of him?"

"Why ask me?"

"Because he stopped here yesterday. He didn't say so, but I know he did."

"Where did you find him? I mean, did he go to your camp?"

"He was lucky—he didn't make it that far. He wolfed it out last night by a fire in the timber about two miles short of Old Camp."

"What happened to his horse?" Casey asked.

"He turned it loose, figuring it might have a chance to come back here. It piled up in a drift and froze plumb to death, standing."

Casey felt the strike of pain. That big, beautiful, strong horse . . .

"What did you make of Gibson, I asked." Pa cocked his eye.

"He seemed determined."

"Determined to what?"

Casey looked at her roast. She tried it with a long fork. Just right.

"It beats all, the way you're set to cook everything in the oven," Pa said. "Smells fair, though. Yeah, he was determined, all right. He's dangerous and tough, that fellow. A little less wind and cold and he'd have come right in on us, and then I don't know how I would have kept the boys from killing him. They was in a bad temper, anyway. We like to froze in that cabin, except Eldon. He's like a bear when it comes to sleeping—and snoring."

And trying to make love, Casey wanted to add. "Then you don't favor killing?"

Pa rubbed the bristles on his throat. "I ain't against it when it's someone like Gibson. He's a sneaking detective, or I've missed my guess a mile. The cattlemen are buying his beans. No, I ain't against killing, but it ain't smart. First thing you know, you've got a bad reputation."

"What are you going to do to Gibson?"

"Do to him?" Pa laughed. "Why, I'll feed him just like anybody else that comes around, lend him a horse, and let him go right back to Chamberlain and Armbruster and old Stan Meixler so's he can tell 'em he didn't do no better than the others at catching Joel Bragg. What did you think I was going to do with him?"

Greatly relieved, Casey said carefully, "I thought you might shoot him."

"If I wanted him killed, I would have busted his leg and left him right where we found him wallowing in the snow. Harve and Eldon was of a mind to do just that, and I thought on it a minute or two, but that wouldn't have been near as good as letting him go back to the crooks that hired him, with a can tied to his tail."

The crooks? Wrong was always on the other side, of course, but Pa was a smart man who openly admitted his thievery. He must think he had some good reason for calling the cattlemen of the area crooks. "Mr. Penfield was here yesterday."

"Oh?"

"He came to warn you about Gibson."

Pa got a mean look. "Why didn't you tell me right off?"

"Well, I saw that Gibson was with you, and I thought—"

"You thought I knew who he was, huh? How would I know that?"

It was an uneasy moment. Pa was really mad. "No one gets around you, Mr. Bragg. I was sure that Gibson hadn't fooled you one bit."

"Woman, you're trying to get around me right now!" Pa yelled, but he was somewhat mollified. "After this, by Ned, don't waste no time telling me what I ought to know."

"All right, I will not withhold any information which I think you ought to know," Casey said.

Pa groaned. "What a sneaky answer!" He shook his head. "Women that can use words . . . they'll kill you dead." His scowl was as ferocious as ever, but Casey could see that the bite had gone out of him. "You ain't soft on that Gibson, are you?"

Busy at the stove, Casey didn't look around. "Hardly," she said brusquely. "He's not the first good-looking man I've ever seen, you know."

"Yeah," Pa grunted. "Now tell me everything Onreliable said."

Casey told him.

"Did you load Onreliable up with grub?"

"I fed him, yes."

"I mean give him a big sackful of grub from the cellar. I always do that when he does me a favor."

"He didn't ask, and it didn't occur to me." Casey was to learn later that Pa was in the habit of giving a great many residents of the area sackfuls of grub and other items, which helped explain why the law was always one step behind him.

He got up suddenly and began to strop his razor at the washstand. He poured hot water into the pan and peered at himself in a fragment of mirror held to the logs by nails. "So you didn't give him no food. Did you give him anything else?"

"No!"

Pa chuckled. "What did he offer you?"

"I don't care to talk about it, Mr. Bragg."

"I do. I'll bet one thing, he didn't get away from here without trying, did he?"

"Yes, he tried."

Pa grinned. "So?"

"I pushed him into the washtub."

Pa made a stroke in the air with the gleaming razor. "By Ned! I wish I could have seen that! Dumped him in the washtub. You're doing fine, Cissie, if you can just keep it up."

"I fully intend to."

Pa chuckled to himself while he was shaving, flipping hair and lather from the razor toward the woodbox. Some of it hit the wood and some of it hit the walls and floor. Casey ground her teeth. She wanted to get him an old towel to wipe the razor on, but she thought it best to stand for a while on the few small victories she had won before pushing further.

"Have you made up your mind about my staying, Mr. Bragg?"

"I'm thinking on it, Cissie. I'm thinking on it."

Casey was tired from lack of sleep and the strain of the night before. She hoped the Braggs' hard night at Old Camp had taken some of the steam from them, too, but when they came charging in at the sound of the railroad iron, she saw they were just as full of the devil as ever. They were all shining-shaved, and Harve, as usual, had his hair neatly parted and plastered down, with the charming roach effect.

And in the hot room all of them smelled as strongly as ever of old sweat and stale clothing.

145

As they gorged, Harve and Eldon watched Casey with an animal interest that was beginning to be unnerving.

And there was Gibson, a detective who had come close to dying because of his hard-nosed pursuit of them, sitting in their very midst, being treated as if he were any ordinary guest. He did not seem to be any more tense or restless than he had been with Casey alone, but she observed that he did not eat very much.

Just once Eldon, with his mouth full, tried a few heavy-handed jests about Gibson's trapping career, but Pa silenced his son with a harsh stare.

For a man with a touchy stomach, Pa ate very well. After his second piece of apple pie, he dropped his knife and fork with a clatter and said, "Back to the bunkhouse."

Eldon was caught short. Casey had just served him a third portion of pie. He scooped it up in his hand and ate it on the way to the door. Leaving slowly, Harve bumped against Casey and got in a little pat. "I guess maybe I'll help with the dishes, Pa."

"Fine, Harve boy, fine!" Pa said. "You can do that the very day your ma and the girls get back. Now git!"

Pa herded them all out, and then he followed them.

Casey had baked six loaves of bread. They were gone, except for the half loaf she had put in the pantry. Everything else was cleaned up, too.

When she went out for snow, she heard music in the bunkhouse—a violin, a banjo, two mouth harps, and a jug. There was a lot of enthusiasm in the effort, if not perfection. Then Thum and Cougar began to howl. The music stopped, and the Braggs laughed, and someone opened the door and let the dogs out.

With the dishes stacked, Casey was waiting for the water to get hot when Pinky came in. "Pa said for me to get some water and wood."

"Why, thank you."

"He sort of trusts me, you know. You can trust me, too, Miss Casey. I ain't like Eldon and Harve. It's not that I don't—I'm glad you didn't tell Pa what happened at Overton's."

"There was no need for him to know."

"Yeah. I had a bad enough time with everybody on the way to Old Camp and while we was there, over that miserable sorrel horse."

"I'll bet you did, Pinky. Did you leave the horse there?"

"Oh, sure. We got a shed up there, and there's some pretty good grass on the ridges where the wind blows the snow away. We got a few of our own cows there, too. Our own." Pinky shuffled his feet. "Well, I better get busy."

He filled the woodbox and brought two buckets of water and asked if there was anything else he could do. Casey said she guessed not.

"If Pa ain't around sometime and anything starts to happen, you yell for me, Miss Casey."

"I will. Thank you."

"I've got to get back now, but you remember what I said."

The weakest of them all, her self-appointed protector. Casey did not find it amusing. She took a small measure of self-respect from it.

She looked around the kitchen. It was incredible that men could consume food the way the Braggs did. They would be back for supper in a few hours. It would have to be steak and biscuits and canned fruit. The Braggs didn't need a cook; they needed a butcher and a baker.

Pa came in while Casey was broiling steaks for

147

supper. Once more he grumped about her way of cooking. "That's the queerest way of frying meat I ever seen."

"You ate it before."

"A man eats anything when he's up against it, even cougar meat."

In spite of his complaint, Pa was secretly pleased about something, Casey could tell. She did not find out what it was until after supper, when Pinky was attending to the wood and water chores. "Pa, he's a dandy," Pinky said, grinning. "You know what he's going to do to old Gibson? He's going to let him haul a load of beef down to Sap, and we're going to sell it to the woman at the section house, like always. Think of that. This here smart detective comes here to catch Pa, and he winds up hauling stolen beef!"

"How can you make him do it?"

Pinky laughed. "He's got to do it, or walk. He won't know it's stolen meat, anyway. Pa's got a hide around with our own brand on it, from one of our steers we butchered the same time we cut up Chamberlain's stuff."

"That's real clever," Casey said.

Pa would not have missed the sarcasm in her tone, but Pinky was laughing too hard to notice it. "Someday will you show me how to shoot that rifle?" Casey asked, indicating the flintlock above the clock shelf.

"That old thing? Heck, I'll show you how to handle a pistol. I'm a pretty good shot, even better than Boston."

"I don't want to know anything about a pistol. The very sight of one makes me shudder, but that rifle is pretty."

"Pretty old, yeah." Pinky took the piece from the pegs. "I guess it was all right in its day." He grew more

148

enthusiastic as he handled the rifle. "I used to shoot rabbits with this until Boston bought a new pistol and gave me his old one."

He took down the powder horn and shot pouch. He showed Casey how to pour powder down the barrel, how to prime the pan and adjust the flint. "You cup this linen patch around the ball, see? I ain't going to load it, though, not right now." As Casey had observed before, his hands were deft and sure, and there was no hesitation in his speech when he was doing something he understood well.

"Now you take this here ramrod . . ." Pinky faltered. Casey saw him staring at her with his soul in his eyes, and then he blurted, "Miss Casey, you better marry me."

"I hadn't thought of marrying anyone, Pinky."

"You got to. Will you, huh?"

His first concern, she thought, was protecting her from his brothers. No doubt he thought he loved her, and perhaps he did, in a boyish way. But he was being honest, and she did not want to hurt him. He reminded her very much of Billy Carpenter.

"No, Pinky. I like you, but I don't really love you enough to marry you. In fact, I have no intention of—"

"We'll leave here. We don't have to stay around my family. I can get a job on the railroad or something."

"I'm sure you could, but I'm not ready to get married. Not for a very long time."

"That's on account of what people are saying about you, but I don't care about that. Even if it was true, I'd want to marry you, Miss Casey." Pinky gulped and contorted his face, and finally twisted the words out. "I—I—love you."

"Thank you, but no"

"Who is it—one of my brothers? You like one of my

149

brothers better?"

Casey shook her head. "I hardly know them. No, Pinky, there's no man."

He took heart from that. It always bolstered a man's confidence to be assured that he was just as good as the next one.

"Then I'll just wait," Pinky said. "I can do that as good as anybody else. I'll wait and—" He broke off suddenly and began talking about the rifle. "Now this here frizzen . . ."

Casey heard the steps outside, and then Pa came in. "What's going on around here?"

"Pinky has been showing me how to work this rifle."

"Yeah?" Pa eyed them steadily. "Whose idea was that?"

"Mine, Mr. Bragg."

"Might not be a bad one at that. You learn to shoot real good, Cissie, and you can bark a few of these here detectives that swarm around the place day and night. All right, Pinky, you get back to the bunkhouse with me. We can't have no real music without your jug."

Casey was emptying the ash pan sometime later when she heard a clear, deep voice singing. She thought it was Gibson and went a few steps closer to the bunkhouse to listen. It was Harve, strumming the banjo and singing. He had a fine voice, but when Casey caught some of the words to his "Jay Bird" song, she retreated hastily to the house with her ears burning.

Casey slept the night through undisturbed by cold, waking only when she heard Pa's noisy fire-building when it was still dark. Afterward she heard him talking to the dogs outside, and then his footsteps squeaked away. She found no joy in rising at four-thirty on a winter morning, but at least one did not dawdle over getting dressed.

Her hair gave her the most trouble. It was hip-length, fine, difficult to manage by herself. As she put it up hastily, she thought about how badly it needed washing, which in itself was a long chore.

At breakfast she wondered again if she would ever get used to the way Harve and Eldon pawed her with their eyes, at the same time consuming pancakes and bacon like men who never expected to see food again. Pinky had just finished his after-breakfast chores and was warming at the stove when Pa's resounding, "Get around!" rocked the frosty air.

"I got to go now," Pinky said. "Remember, there's a bar for the door. You better use it."

"You'll be gone overnight?"

"Oh, yeah, anyway that."

"Who are you expecting to call?"

"We never know. Just use the bar."

In the cold light of early dawn Casey watched them crunching down to the barn. Where they found mirth at such an unholy hour she could not understand, but something made them laugh. The Braggs rode their horses up the hill, into the trees behind the house, while Gibson drove the tall mules hitched to a heavy sleigh.

After emptying the dishwater, Casey stood at the corner of the house, watching as the Braggs dug meat from the snow and loaded it into the sleigh. They stopped near the house long enough for Pinky to run in with a chunk of frozen loin. "Pa said to give you this." Pinky grinned. "Old Gibson, he fell for the whole thing, hide and all."

Casey doubted that he had been fooled or that Pa thought he had deceived Gibson. It would tickle Pa more to know that Gibson was sure the meat was stolen, with no way of proving it.

While Pinky was running back to his horse, Casey stood in the doorway. Gibson smiled at her for the second time, not bleakly rueful as before, but a brief, quizzical flash with a trace of humor in it, as if he were saying, "Look what's happening to me."

And then he sent the cold-edgy mules plunging away. The sleigh made a hissing sound as it slid through the drifts. The Braggs whooped and laughed.

Gibson would be back, Casey was sure.

# CHAPTER 12

*"That woman—Leclair, you say?—was beyond redemption when I met her. All kinds of evil, wretched females consorted with outlaw gangs or drifted from mining camp to mining camp in those days. I struggled with the devil for the souls of some of them, but I fear I lost far more often than I won."*
R. L. Jimmerson, one-time lay preacher, real estate salesman, Hollywood, California, 1932.

HER MORNING CHORES COMPLETED, CASEY CHARGED THE long rifle, following Pinky's instructions carefully. How men had managed to kill so many other men with such a thing was a puzzle, considering the skill and time required to spill just the right amount of powder down the barrel, to cup the patch around the little lead ball, to shove the whole thing down on the powder, to prime the pan, cock the piece, look down the sights, and pull the trigger.

It seemed like a terribly involved process to Casey. Sometimes after one did everything right, the rifle still wouldn't fire, according to Pinky.

The silver inlays, set into the beautifully polished stock of curly maple, and the silver butt plate were very nice, Casey thought. She admired the delicate chasing on the barrel, too, though the whole piece as an instrument was rather frightening.

But she might need to know how to use the rifle someday; she could not go on forever pushing people into tubs of wash water or putting hot stove lifters down their shirts. Perhaps a pistol would have been better, after all—a little one that didn't make much noise.

She primed the pan and carried the rifle to the doorway, where she sighted vaguely on the meadow. She could not pull the trigger. She found herself closing her eyes and turning her head away from the prospective explosion. Maybe she had put too much powder into it, or something. The whole thing might blow up with a terrible roar.

Quite likely she would never need it, anyway. She pushed the cover over the pan and put the piece back on its pegs. Occasionally, while baking bread, she glanced at the rifle and told herself she was a coward.

Early in the afternoon she decided it was a good-time to wash her hair, though she detested the endless chore of drying it and the fight to work it into a coiffure that would not require constant attention. There was no way to avoid the task without being unclean, and she made the preparations—heating water, laying out combs, towels, her only bar of scented soap, and getting a jug of vinegar from the pantry.

She was ready to begin the operation when the bold idea came. Once it struck her, she acted without weakening her purpose by further consideration. She got Mrs. Bragg's scissors from the sewing basket and began to chop away. Her long tresses fell to the floor around her in honey-colored folds. She cut by feel alone, hacking away until her hair was no more than two inches long all over her head. She could feel stair steps in the back, but the more she tried to trim them smooth, the more ragged they seemed to get.

Afterward she went to her room to see how she looked, but she stopped just inside the doorway, looking at the back of the mirror, and then she turned away from it; she didn't look at herself in the fragment of glass that Pa used for shaving, either.

She probably looked awful, she thought, but she felt relieved of a cumbersome burden. She quickly gathered her fallen hair clippings and burned them in the stove. They made a fearful stench when the lid was up.

And then she washed her hair and laughed out loud at the ease with which she dried it. Pa would be the one who would raise the devil about it.

Spurred on by a feeling of freedom and achievement, she took down the flintlock. At the last instant before jerking the light trigger, she closed her eyes and turned her head away. The sharp crack wasn't much, and there was scarcely any recoil at all. The stink of powder that blew back from the open doorway was the worst part of the experience.

Casey fired the rifle nine more times.

Each shot gave her increased confidence until, to her surprise, she saw that she was hitting rather close to the lone post showing above the snow in the meadow. By then the rifle was becoming fouled, kicking harder on each shot. She cleaned it the way Pinky had instructed, trying to make the barrel gleam "like a diamond tooth in a goat's mouth." Since she could not see down the barrel to judge her efforts, she kept running patches in until they came out clean.

The visitor came in late afternoon while she was waiting for her third batch of bread to bake. She was resting at the moment, having tea and feeling pleased with her accomplishments of that day. For once, Thum and Cougar got the jump on the geese. The dogs were dug in for warmth against the manure pile near the barn. From that vantage point one of them spotted the rider coming up the valley and gave the warning.

Beaten at their own game, the geese tried to make up for their lapse by continuing their racket even after the rider had reached the house.

Another man. One who stared at Casey with a puzzled expression. It would be nice, she thought, if just one time a woman came to visit, instead of the seemingly steady parade of lone, questing males with ideas jumping across their faces the instant they saw her.

This one was wearing a scabby bearskin coat and fur gauntlets with the stitches loose at the fingertips. He rode a poor horse. When he got down, uninvited, Casey noticed how the front of the saddle twisted, as if the fork were broken. Contrasting strangely with his clothes and equipment, the man's hat was almost elegant—a spotless white broad-brimmed headpiece that he wore like a badge of office.

He was another officer of some kind, Casey decided; he had the piercing look of one, and a heavy, jutting jaw stubbled with bluish-black beard.

"Whose child are you?" he asked. His voice was deep and rolling.

Child! Why, the whopper-jawed billy goat with his fancy hat! Who did he think he was talking to? And

155

then Casey remembered her hair. She could not keep herself from running her hand across it.

He needed no invitation to enter the house. He walked in as if he were well accustomed to the place and welcome. "Where is she?" he demanded.

"I am here alone."

"Then where has she gone? I have been sent here as a servant of the Lord to speak to this woman."

Oh! One of those, Casey thought. She had seen them before at Miss Leduc's house, but not as servants of the Lord. "You're looking for Miss Leclair, I assume?"

"I am indeed, child. I am the Reverend Jimmerson, come on His mission to do what I can for a poor, misguided woman. Now tell me where she is."

"You're looking at her," Casey said disgustedly.

A great light dawned on Jimmerson. "You?" His eyes gleamed. "Ah, yes, I see it now. I see the marks of carnal lust, the scarlet stain, the beckoning eye, the—"

"Have you eaten, Mr. Jimmerson?"

That stopped him in mid-flight. "No, I have not broken bread for many hours. My spirit rises above the needs of the body when I am doing His work." Most speedily the Reverend Jimmerson divested himself of his coat and gauntlets, dropping them on a chair. He was more careful about his hat, blowing gently at some trace of dust upon it before he hung it on a wooden peg near the woodbox. He admired it for a moment, and then he seated himself at the table. "Now, what do you have to eat, child?"

"I am not a child, Mr. Jimmerson."

"*Reverend* Jimmerson, please. We are all children, and some of us go astray, and that is why I am here." His burning look followed her around the room.

Casey cut him a steak, a thin one from the shank of

the haunch in the pantry
she had boiled that mor[...]
some of the hard, dark
whose spirit was so much
not mind a few bitter lumps

Jimmerson talked to her [...]
her bread burn.

"You have taken a step in
see you have cut your hair as p

"I cut it because it was a nuis

Jimmerson made a tepee of
fingertips together. "That is wha[...]
heart you know, and I know, tha[...]
debasement."

"Have it your way."

"*His* way, child. *I* am but an instru[...]

Casey remembered her father's
appointed crusaders caused about th
world's trouble. She had one on her ha
jawed and beady-eyed. "What church [...]
Mr. Jimmerson?"

"At the moment—none," he said imp
he were standing in majestic alo
considering the entreaties of mar
congregations for him to come and lead the[...]
of the Lord. "I do His bidding where He ca
strange places."

He had a remarkable appetite. He would ha
full loaf of bread if Casey had not cut him off
what remained of the loaf to the safety of the pa[...]

Jimmerson rose and paced the floor slowly,
meditation, hands behind his back. "We will be
hearing the story of your downfall, child. In it [...]
find some point from which I can begin the wo[...]

salvation."
Casey wa
sparkled in
Jimmerson
middle of
degrading
"I am h
"It beg
young gi
unspoile
After sc
shop,
orname
church
Jimme
everyt
"Ye
"Th
sighe
Ji
Ever
salv
cou
co

s gathering up the dishes. Little devil lights
her eyes as she suddenly decided to hit
where it would confuse him most—in the
his self-righteous pomposity. "It's a long, sad,
tale."

ere to listen," Jimmerson said eagerly.
an in this little church in Ohio when I was a
l. Though I had many beaux, I was a simple,
child who did not know the meaning of life.
hool each day I worked in my father's harness
iling horse collars and polishing the brass
ts on the hames, and every Sunday I went to
in my white dress." Casey paused to see if
rson had caught on. He was swallowing
hing.

s, yes, go on," he said.
here was a man, an elder in the church . . ." Casey
d. "He said his wife did not understand him."
merson licked his lips. "Tell everything, child.
ything! Only then can I begin the work of
ation."

He took up the collection in church. He couldn't
nt beyond ten, so it became my task to help him
nt the money in a little room behind the altar."
"Ah, yes!"

Casey bowed her head. "We began to cheat."

"To cheat? That is an odd word to describe your kind
f sin. You mean you began to—? You tell me."

"We cheated," Casey said. "We took some of the
money and bought hard cider at Grubenhoofer's mill."

"And then?"

"We drank it in the trees behind the mill, swilling it
down like hungry swine, singing gay songs, reading

from the Song of Solomon."

"And then?"

Casey shook her head sadly.

"Tell me, child!"

"Then he—then he . . ."

"Everything, I said!"

"Well, as soon as he had about a dozen swigs of cider, he fell asleep and snored something awful, and I went home."

Jimmerson stared. His mouth was open, his lips drawn away from his long teeth, his whole expression one of eager anticipation. And then he was puzzled, not grasping the fact that he had been taken in. "That was all? Is that all?"

"That's it, the whole pitiful story of my downfall."

"You lured someone else?"

"Oh, no! I never looked at another man after that."

Jimmerson turned white with rage. "You low, foul woman, you've made light of my God-inspired desire to help you! I should leave you straightaway to wallow in your degradation, to suffer the torments, to be damned eternally!"

"Why don't you do that, Mr. Jimmerson?" Casey said cheerfully. She opened the door.

"No! I will not be set aside so easily by the devil." Jimmerson gained control of himself. He went back to pacing with his hands behind him, and after a time he drew upon the Bible. " 'For the lips of a strange woman drop as honey, and her mouth is smoother than oil. But her end is bitter as wormwood, sharp as a two-edged sword. Her feet go down to death; her steps take hold on hell.' Do you hear me, woman?"

"Yes, Mr. Jimmerson. The word is 'honeycomb.' And since you like Proverbs, hear this one, " 'Withdraw thy

159

foot from thy neighbor's house; lest he be weary of thee, and so hate thee.' "

"I will not be driven by evil! You are twisting holy words in an effort to turn me from my mission." Jimmerson raised his hands high and closed his eyes. "I was sent to struggle with the devil for your soul, and I will not turn aside."

"Bosh!" said Casey. "Get out." She glanced at the long rifle on the wall across the room.

"We must pray," Jimmerson announced.

"Go ahead." Casey started toward the rifle.

Jimmerson came forward, arms still raised, and blocked her way between the table and the stove. His hands came down hard on her shoulders, and she felt the sweaty heat of his palms as he gripped her, imploring the Almighty to receive her confession of sin. His prayer was short. His hands kept flexing. "And now I must wrestle the devil for your soul."

After a very brief session of that, Casey was sure that the devil and her soul were forgotten considerations; Jimmerson was wrestling for something else.

She was forced back across the room. The devil went out the window and ardor rushed in. Her back was against the wall near the woodbox, and Jimmerson's hands were seeking evil in strange places.

She got one arm free and grabbed his hat from its peg. She tossed it on the hot stove, brim down. It stuck instantly and began to smoke.

"Jesus Christ!" Jimmerson yelled. He grabbed the hat from the stove and began to beat at the scorched brim. "My crowning glory, my beautiful hat," he mourned.

So absorbed was he in grieving over his hat that he paid no attention to Casey until after she had run across the room and seized the rifle. She poured in powder and

160

rammed a ball home.

Jimmerson put his ruined hat on the table. He unbuckled his belt and stripped it off. "You're going to pay for that, you little bitch!" He was no longer the handpicked of the Lord, but a very angry, white-faced man.

He wrapped the belt around his hand, and then he slapped the loose end against the table with a sharp whack. "I'm going to strap you until you cry in vain for mercy."

Casey got the weapon primed as he walked around the table.

"That won't fire, you fool," he said contemptuously. He snapped the belt. His eyes were curiously blank.

"Don't touch me!" Casey warned.

Jimmerson took another slow step toward her, swinging the belt. The rifle went off as Casey was raising it. She was not immediately sure of what happened afterward. To begin with, she had put too much powder in both the barrel and pan. A blinding cloud of smoke rose in her face. The recoil almost tore the rifle from her grip.

"Oh, God, I'm shot!" Jimmerson cried. He crashed against the door. He jerked it open and stumbled outside.

The angle was such that Casey could no longer see him. She did not want to look, but she forced herself to step over to where she could see outside. Jimmerson was limping back and forth near his horse, rubbing his leg. There was no blood or any other evidence of injury. He must have fallen down when he ran, Casey thought.

She picked his hat off the floor and started to throw it through the doorway, and then she hesitated when she saw two holes in the crown. They had not been there before, she was sure. Jimmerson's belt was lying on the threshold. Casey kicked it outside, and then she tossed the rest of Jimmerson's possessions after it. He jumped quickly to retrieve the hat, letting the other articles lie.

"There has been a great misunderstanding, child. The devil overcame me for a moment, but now I have bested him. We must try once more to—"

Casey slammed the door and put the bar in place. She bowed her head and leaned on the table, shaken, thankful that she had not killed a man.

When she opened her eyes, she saw a splintery gouge in the table. Her bullet had gone through Jimmerson's hat, sliced across the heavy planks, and—she turned her head quickly. There was a hole in the range back, a few inches from the first tapering pipe joint.

She did not care to trace the flight of the bullet any farther or to try to reconstruct the scene to determine how close she had come to Jimmerson.

It was enough that she had missed him. Now he would go away.

But he did not leave. She saw him take his horse down to the barn. Then he went to the bunkhouse, and a few minutes later he came to the woodpile for pine chunks. Casey watched him from the window. After he got his armful of wood, he stood for a moment or two staring at the house.

Casey cleaned the rifle and reloaded it.

Jimmerson made himself comfortable in the bunkhouse. His leg was still hurting where he had rammed it against the corner of the table when that harlot with the face of an innocent child had tried to kill him. Perhaps he had been too hasty. Perhaps he should have prayed louder and longer and let the spirit enter into her more before he made his move.

But the feel of her young body had upset him and built a mighty fire within him sooner than he had expected. His hands flexed at the memory, and he stared into space with his mouth open.

She was a harlot in a den of thieves. What right had she to turn him away? If she were anything else, Joel Bragg would not have let him come on to the ranch after they met on the road that day. Ever since Bragg's daughters started to grow up, the old bandit had taken a hard and narrow view of Jimmerson's visits.

But he had not turned Jimmerson back today.

"Why, sure, preacher," he said with a serious face, "you just go on up to the place and see if you can help her any."

And big Eldon, the brutish one, had grinned slyly at his brothers. Oh, she was the plaything of the Braggs, no doubt, which made it all the more infuriating; a fallen woman in a lair of wicked men—and she had refused the advances of R. L. Jimmerson.

It was the supreme insult.

And she was so young for one of her kind, so well-formed, so beautiful of face, so exciting to the touch.

Jimmerson paced the floor restlessly.

Before dusk Casey carried in wood for the night and filled the wash boiler with crusts of snow, keeping one eye on the bunkhouse while she worked. Generally a very light eater, she had no desire at all for food when suppertime came, but she forced herself to eat a small bowl of stew, without lighting the lamp over the table.

Jimmerson called to her as she was finishing the meal.

The bar across the door fitted loosely in its brackets,

163

allowing the door to come back an inch or more before striking. Casey looked out at Jimmerson through the crack. He was standing a respectful distance from the step, hat in hands.

"Yes?" Casey said.

"I'm sorry, Miss Leclair, about what happened." He smiled ruefully. "I have all the weaknesses of any man, but I assure you I really meant no harm. It won't happen again, for I've been over there all afternoon asking God for forgiveness. I know He understands. Now, will you forgive me?"

"All right." He really did sound contrite.

"May I come in?"

"What for?"

"Just to talk a few minutes." Jimmerson smiled. "I would like a cup of coffee, too, if it wouldn't be imposing too much."

"It would, Mr. Jimmerson. Good night."

Jimmerson nodded. "I can't blame you, I suppose." He bowed his head and began to back away. "Good night."

The pale light from the snow caught his face as he turned. Casey saw his eyes fix on the window for an instant with a wild intentness, and then his back was toward her and he was walking away slowly with bowed head. She wondered then if she had imagined something about his look that was not there.

It could have been the light. He really had seemed sorry about his behavior. But Casey was uneasy. She did not want to light the lamp; but it was silly to stumble around in the gloom, to cower before a fear that might not be real.

She lit the lamp above the table.

From Pa's room she got the latest issue from a stack

of newspapers he kept on a shelf. It was only a month old. She read that in New York harbor, in October, President Cleveland had dedicated the Statue of Liberty. It was a very large statue, Casey gathered from the description in feet and inches. One could go clear to the top of it by walking up a winding stairway inside. The writer said that, although it was a fine piece of work, the statue might well prove a hindrance to navigation, since pilots of ships possibly would grow so interested in looking at the torch that they would forget their duties and bash their vessels into each other with resulting loss of life and property.

Suddenly Casey found herself staring at the window in the end wall. The day had been warmer than usual, so the small panes were not yet frosted over clear to the top. Only in her room were there curtains. She could hang blankets over the windows, she thought, and then she rebuked herself for conjuring up unnecessary fear.

A self-styled preacher who had tried to do what every other man who came around had tried to do? He was only a man, another man.

She tried to read some more. Her nerves jumped each time the house creaked from cold. Slowly she walked through the rooms, looking at the windows. All of them were solidly set, not made for opening. Each time she turned her back, the window she had just examined became an eye staring at her.

At eight o'clock she stoked the fire and went to bed. For a long time she listened to the normal noises that always came with the contraction of the house. Her nerves had betrayed her, she decided. Her fears had been groundless.

She slipped quickly into peaceful sleep.

The scratching noise that woke her sometime later

was not one of the usual sounds that came from the cold. She pulled the blankets away from her ears, and she knew at once by the chill of the room that long hours had passed since she'd fallen asleep.

The noise was in the main room, the raking of something against wood. Quietly she rose and walked in her bare feet across the cold planks until she was at the stove, and there she felt an icy draft flowing against her legs.

The door had been pushed back against the bar. Jimmerson was out there, trying to lift the bar with something he had thrust through the crack. She could hear the heavy sound of his breathing.

She groped carefully on the table for the rifle. Before retiring she had considered taking it to her room, and then she had told herself that to do so would be an expression of fear, and at the last moment she had put in on the table. Her fingers touched the cold barrel and closed around it with a convulsive movement.

"Mr. Jimmerson, I'm going to shoot through that door in three seconds!"

Something dropped on the floor. She heard him run. And then he cried out in a voice quavering with rage and frustration, "You strumpet! You bitch!"

He was standing there in the clear starlight when she jerked the door open and raised the rifle. It made a sharp snap as she cocked it.

Jimmerson ran toward the bunkhouse, whimpering as he scurried down the hard-packed trail.

Casey lit the lamp. It was one o'clock. She built the fire and sat for a while with her feet on the oven door. She doubted that he would try again, but as a precaution she wedged sticks of kindling between the door and the bar. It was then she found the slammer for the dinner

166

signal lying on the floor.

And then, while putting the rifle on its pegs above the clock, she discovered there was no priming in the pan. It would not have fired. A broken reed on which she had placed all her trust. That was when she began to doubt the value of her behavior ever since she had been at the ranch.

For another hour she sat before the fire thinking about it. She had protected herself against the mauling of men by violence and trickery, and, on the surface, it had all worked out well enough, but what solid gains had she made, except respect from Pinky? Even that possibly was more blind puppy love than genuine respect.

She could not go on the rest of her life waging a physical battle. It was not a woman's way; it was only temporary expediency that had been forced on her by circumstance. Eternal vigilance was all right for geese, but not for her.

The bleak, dead hours of early morning put a dreary cast upon the future. She was a frightened child suddenly realizing that life was a grinding process, that human beings were the lowest form of life on earth, remembering error in their fellow beings above all else.

Sometime later, like a weary youngster who has tried hard to stay awake until a late hour, lest he miss some great pronouncement by his elders, Casey stumbled off to bed, where sleep resolved all problems for a while.

When she rose a few hours later, she knew that something from the night before had changed her thinking. She no longer wanted Jimmerson to go away without first seeing him. If she let him go without facing him, he would carry beyond recall part of her problem.

As soon as she had cooked breakfast, she sounded the signal. Jimmerson did not respond. She could see smoke

167

from the bunkhouse stovepipe, so after a short wait she walked over close to the building and called him.

He opened the door and peered out doubtfully, his hair on end, his face haggard, as if he had not slept.

"Breakfast, Mr. Jimmerson," Casey said.

"You mean me?"

"Why, certainly. Who else is in there?"

"Nobody. But I didn't think—that is, I wondered—"

"It will be on the table in five minutes," Casey said brusquely.

Jimmerson knocked when he came to the door. He was still doubtful when he entered. Casey pretended not to see his quick, uneasy glance at the rifle on the wall. She gave him a chair at the end of the table, seating herself on the side next to the stove. Jimmerson looked around uneasily, not quite meeting her eye.

"Will you say grace, please?" she asked.

Jimmerson stammered over the words.

Casey ate as if nothing had happened the night before, talking unconcernedly about the weather, the geese, and the fact that she was going to bake bread that day, since the Braggs were such heavy eaters. Jimmerson nodded and mumbled polite words and hurried through the meal like a man who was late for a vital appointment. "Are you kin of Joel Bragg?" he asked.

"No."

"Or Mrs. Bragg?"

"No, Mr. Jimmerson."

"I see," he murmured, perplexed. "Are you going to marry one of his sons?"

"No."

"You—you merely cook here? I mean—"

"You're beginning to grasp the truth, Mr.

Jimmerson," Casey said evenly.

He winced under her direct look.

"If you're going to wait for Mr. Bragg, I'll have to ask you to use the bunkhouse, since I have a great deal of work to do here."

Jimmerson rose. "I'm not going to wait." He gestured vaguely. "I, too, have work to do."

He rode away soon afterward, back down the valley.

He was more confused than converted, Casey thought. She had not gained any lasting respect from him, nor could she ever from his kind, but she had gained some respect for herself by winning the last meeting with him on the basis of her character, not by violence.

# CHAPTER 13

*"Sure we bought stolen beef. I worked in a lot of mining camp butcher shops, Monarch, Leadville, Cripple Creek, Montezuma—a lot of places. Miners and prospectors never thought cattlemen were the lords of creation, and the other way around, too. If you just happened to make a nighttime buy on a pack train of beef, you didn't waste time asking questions. We bought a lot of wild game, too, but there wasn't any law about that, or not much, at least."* Sim Wallace, retired butcher, Garfield, Colorado, 1921.

PA AND THE BOYS CAME HOME LATE IN THE AFTERNOON two days after Jimmerson's departure. They had at least one beef left, for Casey saw Pinky and Boston with the sleigh in the trees on the hill behind the house, unloading meat and storing it in the snow.

Pa came up from the barn a few minutes later. "Well, Cissie—" he said, and then he roared, "What in the name of Jehoshaphat have you done to your hair!"

"I cut it."

"You scalped it!" Pa slammed his hat on the table. "You've gone and ruined yourself. Shameless, shameless! What made you do such a thing?"

Casey had never seen him so worked up. "It'll grow back."

"First you wear men's pants, and then you cut your hair like a fly-up-the-crick. What will people say about you?"

If he hadn't been so mad, Casey would have found his last remark laughable. She kept quiet while he stomped around the room and ranted. He ran down at last, though every time he looked at her he shook his head. "You keep that kind of thing up and you're going to give this ranch a bad name." After a spell of pure glaring, Pa threw his hat toward a corner of the room and heaved his sheepskin after it.

He began to shave, flipping lather from the razor toward the woodbox.

"I hung an old towel there to wipe the razor on," Casey said.

"I see it! You think I'm blind? I wondered how long it would be before you got guts enough to tell me." Thereafter Pa used the towel, except for occasional lapses. "I had three shaves in Gunnison. That barber don't know nothing."

"Where's Gunnison?"

"Jehoshaphat, girl, you went through there on the train!"

"All I remember is the name."

170

"County seat," Pa growled. "Full of crooked politicians. They had one good man there a few years back, Joe Cotter, the treasurer. Because he was a Republican, the others lied about him, so he had to take some of the county money and get out of town."

"How much did he take?"

"All of it. Served 'em right."

Some of Pa's ideas about right and wrong were most confusing, Casey thought, and when mixed with politics they became completely baffling.

"We went to town for a little spree, sort of. I thought it would do the boys good." Pa turned, gesturing with the razor. "Eldon was in jail one night for fighting. Somebody tried to slice Harve with a knife over a woman, and Pinky had to hit the fellow with a chair. They had a time, though. Trouble is they was like young bulls again by the time we got back on the train." Pa shook his head. "Hardly pays to take 'em to town." He cocked one eye. "You want to marry one of them, Cissie?"

"No."

"Boston wouldn't give you too much trouble."

"They all have their good points, Mr. Bragg. I just haven't thought of marrying."

"Yeah." Pa went back to shaving. While he was drying his face, he asked, "How'd you get along with the preacher?"

"All right."

Pa sat down at the table. He glanced at Casey's hair and shook his head. Then he looked around the room and said, "You keep pretty busy, I see, wearing out the floor scrubbing it three times a day."

"Not quite that often, Mr. Bragg."

"Got along fine with Preacher Jimmerson, huh?" Pa

171

tilted his chair and put his hands behind his head. "You call shooting his hat off getting along fine?"

Casey stared at him. "You saw him in town?"

"Nope. Folks at Sap seen him when he come sneaking in with a couple of holes in that fine white hat of his. He acted like a whipped dog." Pa looked at the bullet gouge in the table and the hole in the range back. "Which shot was that?"

"There was only one. His hat was on the table. The rifle went off accidentally."

Pa brought both hands down on his knees and rocked with laughter. "Accident, huh?" he said in a choked voice, and laughed some more. "Cissie, you're a humdinger."

"It wasn't funny, Mr. Bragg!" Casey said. "I might have killed him. I don't appreciate your letting him come here, either, when you knew I was alone. You certainly must know what kind of cowardly sneak he is. No doubt you and the boys were laughing about him coming here, and I suppose all the filthy-minded men in Sapinero were making bets about what would happen. I don't know anyone in this country, but they all seem to know about me and everything that happens up here."

Casey was so angry she was close to tears.

"Hmmm." Pa studied her face. "Maybe it wasn't such a smart stunt, after all." It was about as close as he had ever come to an apology. "I knew you could handle him, though."

"I don't want to go the rest of my life 'handling' men!"

"Then you shouldn't've cut your hair like that!"

"It was my hair!"

"Shut up!" Pa roared. "I ought to put you across my knee and whomp you. You ain't too old to be licked."

172

He stomped around the room, snatched the rifle from its pegs and went outside with it. He held it close to the snow, leaning down to squint into the barrel. He came back in and put the weapon on the wall. "Clean. How'd that happen, I wonder."

"Because I cleaned it," Casey said sweetly.

"Always bragging," Pa growled. "You probably even think you bake bread fit to eat. I think I'll try some of it before the hogs get in here."

They called it the January thaw. It seemed like a miracle to Casey to find the days suddenly sunny and warm, the snow settling to a third of its former depth, and bare spots appearing on the hills. Harve built a short walk of boards before the step, so that everyone could knock most of the mud off his feet before entering, mud that thawed in the yard every day by ten o'clock and froze again by six.

It was Harve who had built the chairs and dresser in Casey's room, she was surprised to find out. He had made the furniture from aspen logs long immersed under water in beaver ponds, and that, he explained, accounted for the exotic streaks of color in the wood. "If you need anything more in your bedroom, I can supply it," Harve said, and then he actually looked embarrassed, but he recovered from that quickly enough and grinned. "The way I *didn't* mean it ain't a bad idea, at that."

Casey wanted to laugh, but she gave him a cool, disapproving look; her position was not strong enough to allow the luxury of banter on touchy matters.

During the warm spell, which lasted nearly three weeks, she moved freely about the ranch during the daytime. Pa kept the boys busy from morning till night, enlarging the corrals and building a pole shed. Since the Braggs had no cattle, except the ones Pinky had said were at Old Camp, Casey speculated about the improvements, but asked no questions. She learned a great deal of Pa's activities and plans from incidental talk and tried to forget it all as soon as she heard it.

She liked to feed the geese each morning, making friends with some of them, though the gander did not warm up to her beyond toleration. She had just returned the feed can to the sack in the storeroom and was leaving the barn one morning when she heard a noise behind her and saw Eldon coming out of the gloomy shadows of a stall.

He was grinning hideously, his big eyes bulging, his hands extended. Desperately she looked around for a pitchfork as she backed toward the door.

"I got you now," he said.

"Eldon! Eldon, you stay back!"

He kept coming toward her, reaching out. "You ain't got no hot stove lifter this time, Cissie."

Casey's groping fingers touched the latch. She slid it back as Eldon jumped toward her. She slipped through the door and swung it back in his face and ran up the path toward the house. Eldon came pounding along behind her, and she knew he was gaining. She gathered her skirts and tried to go faster.

"Run, little rabbit, run," he said.

She looked over her shoulder in desperation. There he was, like some monstrous, crushing evil. Her backward glance caused her to run into the hard snow beside the path. She staggered and fell.

"Got you!" Eldon roared.

"Pa!" Casey wailed. "Pa, help!" She scrabbled along on hands and knees, and then fell flat on her face.

174

For some strange reason Eldon didn't catch her. She looked around, and he was standing there ten feet away, laughing, and the rest of the Braggs were hanging on the completed side of their new corral, also whooping with laughter. "You beasts!" she yelled. With as much dignity as she could muster, she walked on up to the house.

"Pa!" someone cried in a high voice. "Help, Pa!"

After she got her composure back, Casey had to smile about the incident. She should have known better from the first, she thought, but Eldon had looked so frightening. She had known the others were somewhere close, but still he had scared the living daylights out of her.

That night at supper she gave Eldon a cup of coffee mixed about equally with vinegar. He gulped down one mouthful, frowned, and tried a second one before he strangled and had to run outside.

"Choke, little rabbit, choke," Casey said.

Eldon's brothers and Pa thought it was a tremendously good joke, and Eldon himself took it good-naturedly after he got his breath back. Casey guessed she was catching on to the Braggs a little bit.

"Folks clean down at Sap could have heard you squeal today," Pa told her. "Eldon's sisters used to tease him when they was little to get him to chase them like that so they could yell their heads off."

Though it had been in fun and Casey had accepted it as such, she was sure that any sisterly feeling Eldon might have for her would disappear quickly if he ever found the circumstances favorable. And yet she thought that things were getting to the point where she could handle, as Pa put it, Eldon or Harve, even if Pa wasn't around.

Big animals like Eldon and lady-killers like Harve were sometimes easier to control than, say, men like Boston, who were not so easily understood. He was the last of the boys to leave after supper. He paused at the door and grinned at Casey. "Pa, help!" he mimicked. Casey found herself smiling back at him.

She was beginning to feel sorry for Pinky, who no longer had a monopoly on the chores of carrying wood and water and emptying ashes. He resented the fact that his brothers crowded him aside whenever they could, but was little Casey could do about it without making his position worse.

While the good weather lasted, Casey took advantage of it to do a task she had planned for some time: rearranging and taking stock of the supplies in the storeroom. "I don't see no sense in it," Pa said. "Whatever's there is there. You can always find it if you dig deep enough."

Still, he moved the heavy articles for her, the sacked items and crates, laying everything on the floor by the back wall of the kitchen. When it was all there, Pa shook his head. "I didn't realize there was such a powerful swad of stuff in there. Between buying and getting, I really stuffed that pantry."

"How much of it did you buy?"

"Umm." Pa twisted his mouth. "Some of it."

Though Casey had determined not to see, hear, or have any part of Pa's illegal activities, she removed and destroyed all shipping identification on the supplies before returning them to the storeroom. Pa stayed her hand once when she was putting a strip of broken crate into the stove. The light board was stenciled with "Moses Bloch Mercantile." "That's something I *bought*," Pa said, "whatever it was." And then he

176

shoved the strip into the fire.

Later Casey heard him giving certain orders to the boys, and there was a general cleaning out of things in the bunkhouse. Eldon carried some crates up from the barn, demolishing them at the woodpile, afterward taking the scraps of wood to the bunkhouse for kindling. Pinky came in and helped Casey move the supplies back into the storeroom. He told her Pa had said to remove the tweed cloth from the walls of her room.

"How long has it been there?" Casey asked.

"Just before my sisters left. Ma didn't want them to tack it up because it was stole in the first place. She gets a little tired of us swiping things." Pinky shook his head. "Sometimes I do, too."

It made a good opening for a moral lecture, but Casey refrained from saying anything.

"Now if you was to marry me," Pinky said, "then—"

"Let's get at that cloth."

They took the tweed down and rolled it back into bolts, which Pinky carried into Pa's room. Casey knew where it went from there, but that was a secret she had discovered accidentally and had never mentioned to the Braggs. She asked no questions and pretended that she did not know where Pinky had hidden the bolts.

Once started on the campaign of eradicating and concealing evidence, Pa was thorough. Casey saw Harve and Boston burning hides on a bonfire in the new corral. The next morning when she went to feed the geese, she observed changes in the storeroom in the barn and noticed that some of the saddles that had been there previously were gone.

She was not snooping into their hiding place when she climbed into the hayloft; she went there at times because the odors and the feel of the loft were reassuring to her in a nostalgic way. She was standing there leaning on a pitchfork and daydreaming when Pa came up the ladder and stuck his head above the floor. For a while he did not say anything.

"You sort of like this old loft, huh, Cissie?"

"Yes. It reminds me— Yes, I do."

"You had a home?"

"Oh, yes."

"Not an orphan, huh?"

"No! What made you think so, Pa?"

"Just the way you bristle up sometimes, I reckon." Pa's face was quizzical and sharp in the half-light coming from under the shingle overlaps. "You ain't near as old as you've made out."

"I'm not?"

"You ain't a day over twenty-one, if that. I'd bet my best saddle on it."

"You might lose your best saddle, too."

"Hah! I've raised a couple of daughters, Cissie, and I grew up with six sisters, so I ain't altogether an idiot when it comes to figuring out how old women are from the way they act."

"You're hard to fool, I'll admit."

"You had me wondering for a spell," Pa allowed, "but I reckon I figured out your little act."

"Oh? And how have I acted?"

"Like an ornery little pup that finally found a home," Pa said. "How long since you had a home, Cissie?"

"Several years."

"Yeah." Pa climbed down. He was kicking around the ashes of the bonfire when Casey left the barn.

He had struck shrewdly at the truth, Casey thought. Until she came to the Bragg ranch, she had regarded everything she did and every stop she made as

178

something temporary, merely a delay before the next jump that would surely be the answer to all her needs and longings. It was strange that here, where she had been warned not to come, where she could never hope to overcome the obstacles that faced her, she still felt the touch of home, in spite of knowing that it was again only a short stop on the way to somewhere else.

Moving about, in itself, was not the fault; it was lack of meaning and stability that she had carried within herself from place to place that had taken her headlong into mistakes. She knew that now. The past could never be retrieved—or entirely forgotten.

But if she left the Braggs with their respect, no matter what the countryside said about her, she would also take with her a growing measure of respect for herself. That must have been what she'd wanted so badly, and was afraid she could not gain, when she hesitated at the final turn of the road there above Cimarron.

She wondered now how much longer it would be wise to stay with the Braggs.

One morning at breakfast Pa announced that the weather was about to break. "We got about three days left. We're going to clean out that beef at Old Camp. I been uneasy about that cache ever since Gibson was here. They'll figure this time to catch us during a storm, but we're going to use that storm to get our licks in first.

"Harve, you're going to stay here. We'll need your horse and the mules, too, to pack everything." Pa looked around the table, ready for a challenge.

Eldon jerked his thumb toward Harve. "You mean you're going to leave *him* here?"

"Him," Pa said.

Harve himself seemed the most surprised. His

179

brothers were downright outraged, Pinky most of all. He said, "Harve's horse don't pack so good, Pa. Now mine, he—"

"Him," Pa growled. "That's the end of it."

Harve looked at Casey. His gold tooth gleamed. "Well, now, I think I—"

"I know what you think!" Eldon pulled his elbow back. "I got a notion to knock all your pretty teeth right down—"

"Shut up!" Pa roared. "Now get out of here, all of you, and get things ready. We'll leave right after dinner."

"Oh, boy," Boston groaned, "another night in that ice hole, with old Eldon snoring his head off."

"He snores in the bunkhouse, too," Pa said.

"Yeah, but I ain't wide-awake and freezing over there."

"The trouble with kids these days is they're all soft-handed and spoon-fed," Pa growled disgustedly. "Now get around!"

Onreliable Penfield showed up in mid-morning. He talked to Pa in the bright sunshine at the corrals for some time before coming on up to the house. "I see you ain't washing this time," he said, grinning.

Casey poured him a cup of coffee. "We'll have dinner in a couple of hours, Mr. Penfield."

"Oh, I can't stay. I'm going on up with Joel and the boys and then get back home." Onreliable stood by the stove drinking his coffee and sucking his mustache.

"You mean they're leaving right away?" Onreliable must have brought disquieting news.

"Right away. I just come by to tell you Joel said for you to fix me up a sack of stuff. Last time I forgot."

"I know." Casey selected items from the pantry and
180

put them into a gunnysack. "How has the weather been over your way, Mr. Penfield?"

"Like anywhere, I guess." Onreliable put his cup on the warming oven. He stood with his sack of loot, fidgeting. "The winters seem to get longer every year, over there by myself. It ain't a bad place. Be worth something one of these days if I keep on working at it." He nodded. "It's most all fine meadowland. I guess you could figure there's only about thirty acres in all on the hill. Right in between old Ross and Armbruster like that—it's going to be worth a heap more than I first thought."

"I certainly wish you luck with your land, Mr. Penfield."

"You do? I sure appreciate that, Miss Casey." Onreliable eyed her brightly. "I've been thinking—if you and me could sort of team up—things would go better. We could build the place up pretty fast. You know." Onreliable shifted the sack from one hand to the other. "That place is going to be worth a lot of money, Miss Casey, and half of everything would be yours."

"Are you proposing marriage, Mr. Penfield?"

"Oh, sure! Sure. Didn't I say so plain as anything?"

About as plainly as he ever said anything, Casey thought.

"Thank you very much for your offer, Mr. Penfield—"

"Then it's settled?"

Casey smiled gently. "I must say no, but I do thank you."

"We could have a honeymoon at the Mullin House in Gunnison for a couple of days and see the sights and—"

"I'm afraid not."

"Oh my." Onreliable shifted the sack again. "A week, maybe? We could have a big time."

181

"No."

"I'll fix the house up any way you want it."

Casey shook her head.

"Buy you a horse, all your own?"

"No, Mr. Penfield."

Onreliable sighed. "I didn't think you'd do it, but I been dreaming, and I thought . . . Well, I guess I better get along now before Joel starts yelling they're ready to go." He took a step toward the door and stopped. "I could go as far as getting you a buggy, a new one with nice yellow stripes on the wheels."

"Have a good trip, Mr. Penfield." Casey ushered him out.

All life was a bargaining game with Onreliable, she mused, but at least he had raised his offer for her: He had thrown in marriage to boot.

She must be making progress.

Fifteen minutes later only Harve was left at the ranch. Casey expected him to come sauntering up to the house at once, all prepared to charm her into submission, but he did not show up until after she rang the dinner signal, and then all he did was eat and go on about his business.

It was rather puzzling. Had Pa given him orders to behave himself? Casey doubted it strongly. Nor did she try to believe that he had changed his attitude toward her, or any other woman he considered fair game.

He worked all afternoon at the barn, coming to the house after sundown to fill the woodbox and carry water, and then he went on over to the bunkhouse to wash up for supper. His approach, Casey was sure, was going to be a considerable cut above instant grappling or pure bargaining.

Harve was going to dazzle her.

She was not disappointed with her conjecture. When

182

he came to supper, he was all slicked up, wearing a brand-new shirt and broad-striped dark pants, and he came bearing gifts—a bottle of champagne and a package loosely wrapped and much wrinkled. And he was full of grace and charm. "After we eat, you can open your gift. I had a hard time smuggling it and this here bottle of champagne back from Gunnison and keeping it hid from the others."

"I'm sure you must have, Harve."

He flourished the bottle. "We'll keep it in a bucket of snow after I open it."

"That's a good idea." Casey felt the bottle while Harve was outside with the bucket. It was warm. Harve came in and plunked the bucket of snow in the middle of the table. "Do you want to chill it a little first?" Casey asked.

"Naw. After I open it we can. Get some tin cups."

Casey also took the precaution of getting a large pan and suggested that Harve set the bottle in it after opening, just in case some of it spilled over. It did not spill; it erupted when he drew the cork. With the exception of what he got on his shirt and pants, the pan caught the overflow, which was about two-thirds of the contents.

"I must have had it too close to the stove," Harve observed ruefully, but, as always, he sprang back from disaster with élan, pouring most of the champagne back into the bottle. Then he pulled out Casey's chair for her and filled her tin cup to overflowing.

They were off to a jolly start with a bucket of snowed champagne between them on the table.

Deferring to the occasion, Harve even slowed his eating to a reasonable speed, though he did toss off cups of champagne like sassafras tea. "There ain't much to

183

that stuff, is there?" he said.

"I find it very stimulating." Casey, who disliked the taste heartily, sipped only a little from her cup.

"You do, huh? I'll be darned." One would have thought the idea had just occurred to Harve. He craned to look across the table. "I notice you ain't drinking too much."

"I'm afraid it will make me completely light-headed."

"It tastes like weak cider to me." Harve had another cupful. He replenished Casey's cup, running it over before he noticed. He sat on the edge of the table. "This is pretty nice, just you and me here enjoying ourselves, a fine meal, champagne and all. Why, we got everything you could find in a—Why, heck, it's just fine."

"Yes, indeed."

"Now you can open your present, Casey."

It was a blue taffeta dress, full-length, well-cut. Casey held it against her. It was very close to a fit, she thought. "How did you know that blue is my favorite color?"

Harve made a grand flourish. "Oh, I just figured it would be. I'm pretty good at that kind of thing." He poured the last of the bottle. "Try it on. Let's see how it looks."

"It needs to be ironed first."

"Yeah, but you can see if it fits and like that. Go ahead!" Harve walked around the table and sat down. "I'll stay right here."

"It's a beautiful dress, Harve, though I don't think you should have gotten it for me. It won't look right with all the wrinkles."

"There's just you and me to see it. Go ahead!" Harve tried to pour more champagne, forgetting that the bottle was empty. "You can iron it later. After all the trouble I had finding something just right and getting it here—"

184

"All right, I'll put it on."

"Now if you need any help—"

"No, thank you. Stay right there."

"Oh, I will." Harve's gold tooth was very much in evidence.

Casey went to her room. The dress was not a near fit; it was perfect. Since she had a tiny waist and unusually wide shoulders for a woman of her size, she wondered how Harve had managed to come up with such an accurate fit. For a moment she was tempted to look into her mirror and do a few pirouettes, but she did not touch the mirror where it stood in blankness behind the trunk. She returned to the big room.

The next step would be dancing. Because of Harve's high condition that would probably not last very long.

"It's a beauty!" he exclaimed. "I don't know how I did it." He rose and bowed. He was a trifle unsteady. "May I have the pleasure of the first dance—and all the others?" He giggled.

He was an excellent dancer, Casey thought, very smooth even on the rough floor where the knots in the planks stood like small hills. One dance was enough for him; he moved on to other interests then.

"No, Harve," Casey said firmly.

"Why not?"

That was a question that could be argued all evening, Casey knew. "Simply because I say no."

"You ain't in a very good position to say no."

"I couldn't be in a better position, because I mean it."

Harve pushed her out to arm's length, holding her with his hands around her waist. "Now tell me the story about the poor, weak little girl and the big, strong man and how he shouldn't ought to force her into something against her will."

185

"That's your story, Harve, not mine."

"Damn you, Casey!" He tried to kiss her. She made no resistance, except to turn her head aside. "What's the matter with you?" Harve demanded. "You took the dress!"

"You can have it back."

"I may just rip it off you!"

"As you wish," Casey said. "You paid for it."

"What's the matter with you, anyway? I don't understand you. You know the kind of woman you are, so why are you pretending to be so nicey-nice? You're not fooling me one damn bit."

"What kind of woman am I?" Casey asked calmly.

"Oh, hell!" Harve flung her away from him. "You came off the line somewhere. It might have been a little more high-toned than most, but it's all the same."

"You know that, do you?"

Harve started to answer angrily, and then he stared at her hard. "You're saying you didn't?"

"You're saying it all."

His face was flushed and angry, and his pride was hurt. "All right, I don't know where you come from, but you pretended to swallow Pinky's lies when you came here, so that pretty well shows what you are."

"I see." Casey nodded. "And how have I acted since I came here, Mr. Bragg?"

Harve went to the stove and jammed wood into it. He dusted his hands and stood there glaring. "I don't have to argue with you, or no other woman. We're here, and you're not going to talk me out of anything, understand?"

"I understand. Then the next step is force? Tell me, is that the way you get all your women, Harve?"

"I never had to force any woman in my life!" he

186

yelled. "There's a dozen of them after me all the time. What makes you think you're so special?"

"Perhaps because I'm not after you, or any other man."

He did not know how to take it. He was still scowling as he went over to the table and sat down, but after a time he forced a laugh. "This is crazy, you and me yelling and fighting. The first time we've been alone together, and we have to act like strange dogs." His confidence began to return, and with it his smile. "I guess some of it is my fault, so let's forget what I said, huh?" He patted his lap. "Come on over and sit down, Casey."

She watched him steadily. "Do you want the dress back?"

"Not if— No!"

"There are no 'ifs.' " Casey went to her room and changed clothes. She folded the blue taffeta, pausing a moment to examine a seam that showed the waist had been altered with thread just a trifle off the shade of the rest of the stitches. She took the garment back to the table and put it into its original wrapping.

Harve watched her silently. The champagne was beginning to strike hard at the Bragg low tolerance for alcohol. He was tipsy, but the high color of his face came more from injured pride than anything else.

"There you are," Casey said pleasantly, pushing the package toward him.

He snatched the dress and lurched to his feet. "You think your particular brand of tail is priceless, don't you? Let me tell you something. One of these days you'll come crawling to me, and I'm going to stand there and laugh." He went out, slamming the door hard.

Casey put the bar in place. Harve Bragg had

confirmed something she had suspected for a long time: The Don Juans of the world were childish men, little ones swinging by their knees from tree limbs, crying, "Look at me! See what I can do."

All at once she felt tired and discouraged, and she wondered if she had accomplished anything that night except to insult Harve's sense of manhood and make an enemy of him.

But she did not reckon on the tremendous resiliency of the childish mind. When Harve came to breakfast the next morning, he was neither repentant nor sulky. He did have a terrible hangover, which he said had not been helped by drinking four dipperfuls of water immediately on rising. "I'm about half drunk right now," he said, grinning. "One more bottle of that cider last night and I might have lost my head altogether and gone so far as to ask you to marry me."

"Now wouldn't that have been terrible?"

"Awful. I wouldn't be a very reliable husband. Too many beautiful women have their eye on me."

"I'm distressed," Casey said. He almost believed what he was saying, she thought, but it was a relief to be able to banter with him.

"I'm sorry for the things I said, Casey."

That *was* a surprise. Harve was wrenching his very being to say that much, whether he meant it or not.

"Of course, I ain't going to give up," he added.

And he did not. Casey had to rebuff him every night and at least twice every day until Pa returned with the boys during a storm on the very day he had predicted foul weather. Pa was elated over his timing. "I don't really expect nobody," he said, "but a storm is a good time for some folks to think they can catch me with a stray steer around."

Snow was still falling at noon the next day.

Pinky came to dinner with the package containing the dress under his arm. He gave it to Casey and said, "I figured to do this sometime when I had a decent chance alone, but since all my sneaky brothers have been pawing through my stuff whenever my back was turned . . . Go ahead, unwrap it."

Harve's face was bland and innocent, as if he knew Casey would not cause trouble by betraying him.

For the second time Casey unwrapped the dress and held it against her. "Why, I think it will fit, Pinky." She could not help glancing at Harve.

"It ought to fit," Pa said. "Pinky spent a fortune telegraphing Ma Jensen to get the size of the dress you left with her."

"It's beautiful, Pinky. Thank you."

"Well, go try it on," Pa growled. "I guess we can wait to eat for a few minutes."

"Yeah, try it on," Harve urged.

Something in his voice and look made Pa turn to stare at him with sudden cold suspicion.

While Casey was changing clothes, she heard Pa rumbling questions, and Pinky's voice rising high in anger, and Harve's voice in smooth denial. The fat was in the fire when she came from her room. White-faced, Pinky was pointing at Harve. "You did, you did! I see it now. And that bottle of champagne you've been hiding is gone, too." He swung around to look at Casey. "He brung that dress to you, and he said *he* bought it, didn't he?"

Casey didn't answer.

"Yeah! I was afraid of something like that." Eldon reached toward Harve.

"Hold it!" Pa rapped. "What happened, Cissie?"

189

"Nothing."

"All right, all right, I did it," Harve said, keeping a careful eye on Eldon. "Just a little joke was all."

"Joke!" Pinky howled. He ran around the table and grabbed Harve by the neck and tried to drag him over backward. The table tilted when Harve's feet came up.

Pa snatched up a bowl of mashed potatoes that was sliding toward disaster. "Get away from the table!" he bellowed.

Harve went over backward and became tangled in his chair, and Pinky beat on him furiously until Harve got up and grabbed him, shoving Pinky away with one hand and measuring him with the other. Before he could throw the punch, Boston hit Harve with his shoulder and knocked him staggering toward the corner. "You heard Pa. Stay away from the table."

Pinky caught Harve going away, landed on him, and bore him down, grunting and flailing.

Pa took a sip of coffee. "Look at that wildcat. Stay on him, Pinky boy!"

Pinky boy was doing his best, but he could not hold his brother down. When Harve got up, Pinky was in a fair position to be slaughtered.

It was then the dogs barked savagely. Then one of them howled in pain. Something rasped against the corner of the house. Pa reached the door a fraction ahead of Casey.

Over Pa's shoulder she saw the men and horses in the yard. Down toward the barn other dark forms were drifting through the storm. Three men holding pistols were coming toward the doorway.

"Well, it looks like we got the whole dirty pack in one motion. Just back up easy, Joel." The speaker was a tall man in a long sheepskin coat. The curled brim of his hat was piled with snow. His grizzled mustache was wet. His eyes, Casey observed, were cold blue, with a merciless, triumphant expression.

Before she backed away from the door, she heard a grunting sound at the corner of the house, and someone said, "Haul him up a little more, Sam. He's catching the logs with his hind feet."

# CHAPTER 14

*"I don't know whether Doc Shores ever went up there or not. He must have sent deputies, though. The cattlemen used to make passes on their own, but they didn't give a damn about stolen railroad property, and, to tell the truth, I didn't care about stolen cattle. There was a fellow named Gibson that worked for the Association, and he one time told me he'd seen crates of stuff with the consignee's name still marked on them. The trouble was there was no cooperation between law-enforcement groups in those days. Everybody stole from the railroad. To make it worse, the railroaders themselves lots of times made a cute little game of protecting outlaws. I'll tell you, catching any petty crook was a fair chore, let alone nailing that damned old Joel Bragg. One time, though, we did hit there all together—and that turned out to be something."*
Billy Joe Spense, former Denver & Rio Grande Railroad special agent, Denver, Colorado, 1930.

THE THREE INTRUDERS WERE IN THE HOUSE NOW, AND the Braggs were caught helpless under the muzzles of two pistols. The third man, dark-bearded, with snow-burned cheekbones that were chips of rawness, eased around the door frame of Pa's room, with his pistol ready. Finding no one there, he checked the storeroom in the same cautious way, and then he went slowly toward Casey's room.

She followed him. "You've got your nerve, mister."

He went in carefully behind the poking barrel of his pistol. "That's all of them in the house, Mr. Chamberlain," he called.

"Go help the others."

The scrabbling noise was still going on at the corner of the house. Casey wiped moisture from the glass and looked through the south window. Three men were standing there in the falling snow, watching Cougar, who was hanging by a rope around his neck, his hind feet digging at the logs for support. Shocked and horrified, Casey saw one of the men reach out and bat the dog's feet away from the logs.

She must not run, she thought. Someone would stop her if she went too fast. She forced herself to walk as she went back to the kitchen. The Braggs were all sitting at the far side of the table. One man was standing by the stove, holding a pistol on them. The tall man— Chamberlain, Casey guessed—had one foot on a chair, his weapon resting on his leg. He stood on the near side of the table, looking at the Braggs with an air of satisfaction.

He glanced across his shoulder at Casey. "We don't need you here, sister."

The heavy butcher knife with which she had carved the roast was lying on top of the warming oven of the range. Casey grasped the handle as she moved behind Chamberlain.

"Hey! Drop that!" the man at the stove shouted.

192

Casey darted past him and pulled the door open.

"Let her go, Smitty," Chamberlain said. "You, Harve, settle back."

The snow was cold on Casey's face as she walked along the cabin wall, holding the knife against her skirts. One of the men said, "Look at that, would you, short hair and all."

"No wonder the Braggs stay home."

Cougar was no longer kicking. His hind legs were hanging free, twitching, but lacking strength to dig against the wall.

She was among the men when one of them cried, "She's got a knife!"

Casey got one swipe at the strangling rope looped over a protruding end log. She cut it about halfway through, and then someone grabbed her arm and hauled her back. "Leave her alone!" a familiar voice said. She heard a blow. She was free again. The second time she sawed at the rope, she severed it. She knelt in the snow beside Cougar and dug at the noose around his neck until she got it loose.

For a few moments she thought he was dead, and then she saw his side heave. Someone was cursing, and the familiar voice was speaking in a low, tense tone. After a time Cougar's spasmodic breathing became regular. He staggered up, his eyes wild. There was still fight in him, for he snarled.

"Go to your house!" Casey said. "Go on now!"

The dog wobbled away toward the hillside cave.

Casey faced the men. There were four of them now. "You're a fine bunch of cowards."

Two of them dropped their eyes before her scorn. The third one was holding his jaw. He stared at Casey balefully. "You've got a big mouth, for a whore," he said.

The man who hit him again and knocked him sprawling in the snow was Dick Gibson. He made no apologies to Casey. "Let's go down to the barn," he told the others. "Get up, Samuels."

One of the others said, "I think you're just about through giving anybody orders, Gibson." But he, like the rest, walked away toward the barn after Gibson hauled the prostrate Samuels to his feet and gave him a shove.

Casey brushed dog hair from her sleeves and looked at the bedraggled hem of her taffeta dress as she went back into the house. "Mr. Chamberlain, you've brought a fine bunch of cowards and fiends with you, I must say."

Chamberlain gave her a contemptuous look. "Get back there in your crib, you floozy."

Deep in his throat Eldon growled something unintelligible. He half-rose from the table.

"Keep coming," Chamberlain said. "Next to Harve, you're the one I'd like best to shoot." There was a wicked eagerness in his expression.

"Hold it, Eldon," Pa said. He looked mean enough himself, and unafraid. "Chamberlain, you son-of-a-bitch, keep your tongue off her."

Smitty, the red-faced man near the stove, swung his pistol deliberately until it was pointing at Pa's chest. "Mr. Chamberlain?" It was a plea.

"No," Chamberlain said. "No, we won't do it that way."

Until then anger had carried Casey, but now the brutal coldness of the situation struck her with terrifying impact. These men had murder in their hearts. All Smitty needed was a nod from Chamberlain, who himself was clearly set on killing.

All at once Casey's mind seemed to go blank. She heard the geese making an outcry and realized that the sound had been there for some time. She saw the open door of the storeroom, and it seemed important to close it. After she closed it, she felt vaguely lost for anything else to do. She leaned against the wall and watched. All that food on the table, getting cold . . . and no one touching it.

The bearded man who had searched the house came to the door. "Nothing doing in the bunkhouse, Mr. Chamberlain. It looks like he ain't here."

"All right. Look around for tracks."

"The way it's snowing, Mr. Chamberlain, I don't think—"

"You heard me, Winters!"

"Yes, sir." Winters left quickly.

Casey's shock began to clear. She realized that Boston was not in the room. He was somewhere in the house, for they all had been there when Chamberlain and the other two crowded in. Winters had searched the place, even to looking under the beds, but—she put her hand to her mouth, as if to stifle an exclamation.

The place between Pa's room and the pantry! Once when she was taking clothes from the nails in the wall she had pulled open a door, two boards like all the others, running from the floor to the ceiling. It had swung out quietly, revealing a narrow room. Determined not to snoop, she closed the door quickly.

That was where Pinky had put the bolts of tweed. And that was where Boston was of the moment.

A man in a Hudson Bay jacket came stomping in. Smitty pushed him an arm's length away when he paused at the stove to remove his mittens and warm his hands.

"What do *you* want, Spense?" Chamberlain said.

"I'm going to look in that famous cellar I've heard so much about. Considering some of the losses of our shippers' goods, I thought—"

"Look and then clear out of here."

Chamberlain's arrogance didn't ruffle Spense. He went over to where Casey was standing in front of the pantry door. He stared at her for a moment, and then he touched his hat. "Sorry, ma'am."

She followed him into the pantry. "Please don't stir everything up."

Spense nodded. He scrutinized the contents slowly.

"Perhaps I can help you if you'll tell me what you're looking for, Mr. Spense."

"How do you know my name? Oh, yeah, Chamberlain just said it." Spense examined the sacked goods with particular care, looking for tags or other identifying marks. He took a lamp from a shelf and lit it and used the light to peer at all four sides of the butcher's block. "Ever see any tweed cloth around the place, ma'am?"

"Oh, sure!" Casey waved her hand airily. "The walls of my room used to be draped with it, but I didn't like the colors."

Spense smiled. "Well, I couldn't expect to get much from you, could I?" He gave up on the butcher's block. "You must bake a lot, I see. That's a real supply of soda."

"Isn't it, though?"

Spense's look was keen, but he smiled. "A lot of canned tomatoes there, ma'am."

"We enjoy them, Mr. Spense."

From the kitchen Pa growled, "You want to see a

store bill from where I got them tomatoes, mister?"

"I'll just bet he has one, too," Spense said to Casey. "I'd like to see it, Bragg," he called. Casey and he went out.

"You're wasting my tune playing with these piddling legal details, Spense," Chamberlain said. "You've had two years to prove something, but you and your high-binding railroad—"

"You've had ten years, Mr. Chamberlain. The railroad doesn't take the law into its own hands. We have to follow piddling legal procedure." Spense's voice was mild, but his manner was rock-steady.

"I had no business letting you come along," Chamberlain said. "I'll give you five minutes more, and then I want you out of here, clear out of here. Understand?"

Casey didn't like the sound of it. Pa's face was like stone. His sons looked at each other quietly, and then Pinky took a quick glance toward Pa's bedroom.

"All right, Bragg, let's see those receipts," Spense said.

Pa started to rise.

"She can get them!" Chamberlain rapped.

"That little box on top of my dresser, Cissie."

On her way from Pa's bedroom Casey saw the edge of the sleeve of one of Pa's shirts pinched into a crack between two boards. In passing she lifted a pair of overalls from one nail and hung them on another to cover the shirt.

"I'll take the first look into that box, sister," Chamberlain said. Satisfied that it contained no weapon, he tossed it over to Pa, who sorted through bills until he found what he wanted. He held it out to Spense.

"Ummm." Spense read swiftly. "Yep, among other

197

things, four cases of tomatoes." He returned the paper. "Now do you just happen to have evidence of purchase of that stove in your bunkhouse?"

"I seem to remember something about that," Pa said. "Yeah! Somewhere in here I've got a bill of sale from a horse buyer who does a little freighting now and then."

"Jug Ears Harris," Spense said. He sighed. "Never mind looking for it. Jug Ears would swear to anything but the truth."

Pa shrugged. "I ain't responsible for the honesty of people I buy stuff from."

Chamberlain rapped the table with his pistol. "Goddamn it, Spense, you've had your little fling! Get back to your railroad."

"I'll look around the place a little more, thanks." Spense touched his hat to Casey and went to the door.

"I said for you to clear out of here," Chamberlain warned.

"I heard you." Spense went out, leaving the door open for a courier just coming up the step.

The next visitor was lean-faced, youthful. His hat brim was drooping with its weight of snow. Stopping just inside the door, he started to remove his hat, and then he felt the snow and dropped his hand quickly. "Mr. Chamberlain, Samuels said to tell you—" He saw Casey then, and his brown eyes showed an expression of mingled curiosity and embarrassment.

"Spit it out, Kevin."

"Well, he said—he said there ain't no hides or nothing else around the buildings down there to make real good evidence."

"Oh, he did, did he? You tell Samuels to keep looking, and the rest of them, too. I'll give them fifteen minutes to turn up something."

198

"Yes, sir." Kevin shifted his feet. "He said tell you Gibson was no good to us anymore, and he was keeping an eye on him, so he sent me."

"That's not news," Chamberlain said. "Gibson never was any good to me, and I don't need Samuels to tell me. Get down there and send him up right away."

"Yes, sir." Kevin stopped suddenly on his way to the door. "Samuels, you mean? Send him?"

"Gibson, you damn fool!"

Kevin took a quick look at Casey before he ducked out on the run.

Pa was a despot, Casey thought, but with the tempering quality of humor. Chamberlain was no more than a tyrannical old cur. He was the coldest man Casey had ever seen. He angered her and at the same time frightened her.

But Pa was not one bit awed by him. "Ross, you've ruined a good meal. How much longer are you going to stand there with your foot on that chair, making a fool out of yourself?"

"Not much longer, Joel, just fifteen minutes by your own clock."

Studying the set, fanatical cast of Chamberlain's face, Casey knew he was not gambling and he was not bluffing. He had predetermined his course before he descended on the Bragg ranch, and now he was going through with it. One could not even say that his timing was off, that Pa had outfoxed him by shrewd guesswork about the storm, for it would not make the slightest difference to Chamberlain that the evidence that had been in abundance a few days before was now all gone.

Oh, yes, his men were out there in the storm ransacking the premises for anything that would prove Pa guilty of stealing cattle, but it really didn't matter to

Chamberlain. Unlike Spense, he was not interested in legality; his law was a personal thing in his mind, and the execution of it was in the rust-speckled pistol on his leg and in the blind obedience he would get from red-faced Smitty and the others at the snap of his fingers.

Merciful God, would he kill all the Braggs after he went through his masquerade? It was there before Casey, but she did not want to believe it. Her eyes strayed toward Pa's bedroom. Boston. Boston was their only hope, and yet she wanted him to stay safely where he was, for it seemed to her that all his intervention could accomplish was his own death and an ensuing bloodbath that the Braggs could not possibly win.

She had always heard that thieves were also cowards, but she could see no cowardice in the faces of any of the Braggs. Not even Pinky, whom she had once thought to be as worthless a specimen of man as she had ever known.

Harve caught her eye. His glance flicked to Smitty and back to her. A few moments later he tried again to convey something to her.

Unhurriedly she started toward the woodbox. Smitty put his left hand against her. "Don't walk in front of me."

"Then move over by the door! The fire is going out, and I'll still have greasy dishes to wash."

"Yeah?" Smitty's eyes were small, red from snow glare. He moved over toward the door, possibly because he realized that his back was too warm. He watched Casey with keen suspicion as she put a stick of wood in the stove, first punching at the embers with the poker. She put the poker on top of the warming oven and walked away.

Harve's expression was a mere flick of an eyelid, but

200

it said: "Good!"

"You know what I think I'll do with you, Ross?" Pa said. "After a while I think I'll take you in to the sheriff for trespass, for waving a gun around at unarmed men— and other things I'll think of later. You're in a bad fix, Ross, and you don't know it."

"No fooling?" Chamberlain sneered.

Pa glanced at his sons. Harve grinned. Eldon gave a couple of grunts of throaty laugh, and Pinky's mouth twisted in a thin-lipped grimace.

"No fooling," Pa said calmly. "I'm not even going to offer you the deal of walking out of here right now and taking your men with you. I ain't even going to give you that. No, Ross, you'll have to go see the sheriff with us. Oh, I don't suppose he'll do nothing, but you're going to look awful foolish when the story gets around."

Pa was so easy and convincing that Casey's mind raced wildly trying to determine what his surprise was. He could not be bluffing; surely he would not even try to bluff a man like Chamberlain. Something that Boston was going to do?

"Same old Joel," Chamberlain said. "Full of hot air."

Pa smiled. He winked at his sons, and then he took a piece of bread, buttered it heavily, and began to eat it with obvious enjoyment.

If he had not jarred Chamberlain, he had gotten to Smitty, Casey observed. Smitty's eyes pinched down to tiny balls of redness. He looked at Chamberlain to see how he was taking it. He watched Pa and the boys suspiciously, and then he looked around the room uneasily. "That there cellar they got, Mr. Chamberlain. Maybe there's—"

"There's nothing!" Chamberlain snapped. "He's trying to bluff."

201

He said it too quickly, too positively, Casey thought. There was, after all, a tiny crack in his assurance. And that helped bolster her own conviction that Pa really did have a plan in mind.

"I guess you know by now, Joel," Chamberlain said, "I'm going to hang you."

"You always were hell for wanting to hang somebody, Ross." Pa crammed the last of the bread into his mouth. He reached out and took another thick slice. His hands were steady as he buttered it. "You going to do it *after* I take you to the sheriff?"

"Goddamn you!" Chamberlain's hand was shaking as he pointed at the clock. "In twelve minutes!"

"Hmmm." Pa nodded. "I'll have time for several more hunks of bread then, won't I? Why don't you try some?"

"Goddamn you, Joel!"

Casey saw the side of Chamberlain's neck pulsing.

The short walk outside resounded hollowly to running feet. Kevin came in, breathing hard. "Mr. Chamberlain—"

"I told you to send Gibson to me."

"He wouldn't come. Him and Samuels got in a fracas. Sam wanted to burn the barn down, and Gibson said no, and then Sam tried to cut him with his knife, and Gibson knocked him cold with his gun barrel." Kevin paused for breath. "We still ain't found no hides or nothing, Mr. Chamberlain."

Never before had Casey seen anyone shudder with rage. She saw it now. Chamberlain's arms and shoulders trembled. His thumb jerked up and down against the hammer of his pistol. His face went livid, then white. He looked only at Pa.

Pa munched bread.

Then, like a man ground down to his last measure of patience, Chamberlain asked, "What were the others doing while Gibson was clubbing my foreman?"

"Well, nothing, Mr. Chamberlain. They didn't like it, I guess, but when the mule kicked Winters, they seemed sort of glad to forget everything while they all tried to see if his leg was busted or not. I guess it ain't really busted, but he sure can't walk on it—not while I was there, least-wise."

"Well, now," Pa said, dribbling bread crumbs, "we sure didn't count for no help on the mules or Gibson, did we, boys?"

The boys shook their heads.

Chamberlain's face was a pale mask , of murder as he stared at the Braggs.

Casey put another stick of wood in the fire, purposely jamming one end against the grate so that she had to use the poker to raise it. When she returned the poker to the top of the warming oven, she left the wire handle protruding slightly over the edge. Though Smitty watched her every motion, she thought he was not quite as suspicious as before.

She went back to her position near the pantry door.

Chamberlain moved out into the room. "Stand where I was, Kevin. Kill the first one that even looks crosswise."

"I—you mean—"

"I mean now, damn it!"

Kevin swallowed. He took a pistol from under his sheepskin and did as Chamberlain directed.

"Look at you," Pa said. "Sucking around Uncle Ross won't get you nothing, sonny. Him and me was partners once, so I know how crooked—"

"Shut up!" Scared and nervous, Kevin cocked the

pistol.

Satisfied that Kevin would follow his orders, Chamberlain walked toward the door of the storeroom. "Get out of the way, sister. You've been pretty worried about something in this cellar, ain't you?"

It was Chamberlain who was worried, Casey realized. Pa's confident attitude had shaken him more than she'd thought. She played it out, glancing over her shoulder at the door, as if frightened. Chamberlain raised his hand. "I said move!"

She stood in the doorway while he went inside. From across the room Smitty said, "Don't get any smart ideas about trying to shut him in there, girlie."

Chamberlain moved carefully between the shelves, peering at walls, stamping on the floor, searching for some secret exit.

He kicked the butcher's block over and looked at the floor beneath it. He swept neatly stacked cans from the shelves and rapped the wall. When he returned to the main room, he tried to take his frustration out on Smitty. "That was a fool idea of yours about the cellar."

"I thought— They said Boston's horse was in the corral with the others."

"Which one of Boston's horses?" Harve asked.

Chamberlain examined Casey's room, even to looking under the bed for a trapdoor. His temper did not improve when he came out and saw the Braggs grinning at him.

Then he tried Pa's room. Casey followed him.

This time Chamberlain moved the bed so he could stamp on the floor to determine if any boards were loose. The outer walls were logs. He gave them scant attention. He felt the nails that held the window shut, and then he stood looking narrowly at the partition between the bedroom and the pantry.

He began to thump the wall with his pistol butt. There were logs behind the boards, and so the sound came back solid, but if he struck the door, only two boards thick . . .

"Will you please help me move this bed back, Mr. Chamberlain?" Casey said.

He looked at her in surprise. "Move it yourself. You ought to know a lot about beds, sister." He raised his pistol to rap the wall where the door was.

"Damn you!" Casey cried. That stayed him long enough for her to jump forward and slap his face. "You're a foul-mouthed beast!"

She retreated as he came forward with his fist drawn back. The pulled-out bed came against the back of her legs. "You've got no right to come into people's homes, tearing into everything, knocking cans off the shelves . . ." Anything to bluster, to keep him away from the wall.

Chamberlain lowered his fist slowly. "Shelves, huh? You can't keep your mind off the cellar."

Once more it was Chamberlain's mind that could not give up a falsely implanted idea. "We'll get him. We'll get him when I burn this place, so you may as well tell me. Where is Boston, sister?"

"In Massachusetts, Mr. Chamberlain."

He struck her then, flat-handedly solidly, knocking her sidewise on the bed. "You goddamn whore!"

Casey's ears were ringing, and the back of her neck was aching from shock. He can't hurt me, she told herself, not with words or blows. As she lay there looking into the furious face, gathering back her conscious abilities, she knew it was true.

Chamberlain started out of the room. He brushed against clothing hanging on the secret door and knocked the garments to the floor, revealing Pa's pistol belt which had been suspended from a nail under the clothing. If anyone jerked roughly at the belt, Casey thought, he might pull the door open.

Chamberlain was outside the doorway when she stopped him. He turned and saw her holding the pistol belt. "You overlooked this, Mr. Chamberlain."

Casey walked forward and handed it to him.

Chamberlain's uncertainty increased when he saw that the weapon was loaded.

"Yes," Casey said, "I could have gotten it when I came in here after the box. Incidentally, I'm an excellent shot."

"Why didn't you try it?"

"Because it wasn't necessary, Mr. Chamberlain."

Chamberlain's eyes strayed wildly for a moment, and he looked like a man who suddenly discovers himself in a terrible trap.

Casey walked behind Kevin. She fed the fire again, and this time Smitty paid her scant attention. "Boston's the only one that could be around, Mr. Chamberlain. Even if he is, what can he do?" Smitty asked.

"Nothing!" Chamberlain said loudly. "Bring everybody up here, Kevin. I'll get this business finished."

"Run fast, sonny," Pa said. "Your Uncle Ross is in a rush to go see the sheriff." He grinned as Kevin scooted through the doorway.

Chamberlain put his foot on the chair again. He tapped his gun barrel on the table. "Joel, I'm going to hang you to that pine tree behind your bunkhouse. I'm going to let your sons see every last kick and slobber you make, and then I'm going to take them to Sapinero to catch a train. I'll burn this place to the ground, and if

206

I ever see any of your sons in this country again, I'll hang them as sure as God made little green apples."

"Soup, mud, and potatoes," Pa said. "Ain't you the one for saying *I*?" Anger started slowly in him, but it built with every word he spoke. "*I'm* going to work with the commission so *I* can get the Utes out of the country. *I* got influence with the government. *I'll* fix it so you can hold this fine piece of land you've took up, Joel, old friend. *I'm* going to do that *I—I—I—*

"And now, you dirty son-of-a-bitch, who's on that land?"

Pa had worked himself into a shouting stage, and that created a doubt in Casey's mind. Maybe he had been bluffing all the time, and now he was afraid.

Chamberlain thought the same way. "Ah! Now I feel better, Joel. You had me worried for a second, I'll admit, but now your bluff has run out, and you're back to the same old whine."

"You ain't got me hung yet, Ross," Pa said, but he had lost the power to make Chamberlain uneasy.

They came up from the barn and from the other buildings, and they stood in the falling snow, waiting. Kevin came to the door. "They're all here, Mr. Chamberlain, except Sam and Winters. They ain't in very good shape, so we left 'em in the barn."

Chamberlain motioned with his pistol. "All right, Joel."

Pa looked around wildly. "Now just a minute—!"

"Get up!"

Pa's mouth worked loosely. He was a picture of terror.

"I—I've got to have a trial."

"You've been on trial for ten years or more. Get up!"

Pa rose unsteadily. "I'll be all right when you get

down to it, but don't let my boys see me being drug to that tree," he begged "That ain't asking much, Ross."

"All right. They're going to see plenty, anyway," Chamberlain said. "Keep 'em here, Smitty, until I yell." He glanced at Casey. "Don't let her loose, either."

Pa clung to the door frame. Chamberlain shoved him outside. Pa took a step or two and then fell to his knees in the snow and began to plead incoherently. Three men came toward him like dark forms of doom in the whiteness.

"Stand back. Don't crowd me, sister," Smitty growled. He was facing the Braggs, with his back to the open door.

Casey heard the telltale patter of dirt falling from between the roof poles. "I can't stand it, I can't stand it!" she cried. "Close the door."

"Nobody asked you to look," Smitty said, but he reached behind him with his foot and kicked the door shut.

Casey set up another wailing lament, but it was too late. The dirt was coming down strongly and there was a crunching noise on the roof. For an instant Smitty had too much to watch. He was opening his mouth to yell a warning to the men outside when Casey hit him on the head with the heavy poker.

She thought it had no effect at all, although the blow jarred her wrist. Then Smitty staggered forward. His pistol dropped on the table, and he tried to grab the table to keep from falling. Eldon was on his feet like a big cat. He caught Smitty by the shirt with one hand and hit him a fearful blow.

Outside, Pa was making frightful cries for mercy.

"Drag him!" Chamberlain shouted.

Eldon grabbed Smitty's pistol and went to the door.

Pinky and Harve had run into Pa's bedroom. Casey saw them open the secret door. Then, directly above her on the roof, Boston shouted, "Drop that six-shooter, Chamberlain!"

She saw Pinky and Harve coming out of the bedroom with rifles.

Outside, Chamberlain and his men were caught flat-footed. Three of them were trying to drag Pa to the hanging tree. The rest, except Chamberlain himself, were looking on with their weapons put away.

Though Boston's rifle was trained on his back from less than fifteen feet away, Chamberlain did not drop his pistol until after he looked slowly at the group of silent men before him. Standing next to Gibson, Kevin started to sneak his pistol from under his open sheepskin. The snow was coming down so thickly that he had a good chance of getting away with it. One shot would have broken the situation wide open.

"No, Kevin, don't do it," Gibson said, his words sharp with command and warning.

It was touch and go for an instant, and then the three Braggs burst from the doorway with weapons, and the hanging bee was done.

Chamberlain hurled his pistol into the snow and looked stonily at Gibson. "You're in with them."

"No. But I'm against you."

Standing in the doorway, Casey thought she saw relief on the faces of Chamberlain's men. Kevin looked as if he were going to cry.

Eldon tapped Chamberlain on the shoulder. When the man turned, Eldon hit him a flat, backhanded slap that knocked him full-length in the snow. "That's for Casey!" His legs wide-spraddled, Eldon picked him up and started to slap him again.

"Leave him be," Pa said. He looked old and tired.

"You heard what he kept calling her!" Eldon protested.

"I said leave him be. He's called everybody that don't lick his boots some kind of dirty name." Pa rubbed his hand across his forehead slowly. He gave Chamberlain a pitying look. "Any man so awful set on hanging another has got things eating on him inside. Turn loose of him, Eldon. You might hit him too hard and put him out of his misery, and that would be too big a favor."

Pa kicked around with one foot until he found Chamberlain's pistol. He picked it up and gave it back to the man, still loaded. "There you are, Ross. You want to settle it like a man, you got a gun in your paw. You can get one shot at me and the boys will blow your guts out, but that would be more honest than what you was trying to do"

Chamberlain was breaking. His hand was shaking as he fumbled the pistol into the pocket of his sheepskin.

"That's what I thought," Pa said. "Go home, Ross, and let those little black, crawling things eat at you some more."

It was the worst stripping-away by scorn and pity that Casey would ever witness. The light went out in Chamberlain's eyes. She saw a jerking in one cheek. He put his hand up to stop the tremor. If Pa looked old at the moment, Chamberlain looked like death itself, a burned-out shell with even the surface fires of hate turned to gray ashes.

But he held his head high as he turned and walked away, and his men averted their eyes from him.

Harve started to collect firearms.

"Never mind!" Pa said contemptuously. He waved his arm at the raiders in a sweeping gesture. Not counting

Spense and Gibson, there were eight of them, only about half as many as Casey had thought when she first saw them moving wraithlike in the storm. "There ain't one in the bunch with guts to kill a rabbit less'n old Ross was snarling at them and prodding them along."

Spense and Gibson glanced at each other. The rest looked at no one as they turned and tramped through the snow after their employer.

Smitty brushed against Casey's skirts, groaning as he rolled over and sat up, holding his hand to the side of his face. "My jaw's broke." He looked at Casey helplessly.

She had forgotten him. Now she knelt beside him, glad to know that she had not cracked his head with the poker.

Eldon came in.

"His jaw is broken," Casey explained.

"Gosh, that's too bad." Eldon grabbed Smitty by the collar, dragged him to the doorway, and threw him outside.

Pa disdained even to watch while the raiders collected their injured. They rode away across the meadow. Spense and Gibson went down the road toward Sapinero.

"You don't think they'll come back?" Casey asked Pa.

"Sometime, maybe. If it had been Armbruster and Meixler, things wouldn't have gone so easy. Of course, them two don't go around trying to hang people." Pa frowned. "Maybe I ought to quit stealing cattle and things for a spell or even give it up altogether." He thought a moment. "But the country sort of expects it of me."

"I think you got your revenge on Mr. Chamberlain

today," Casey said.

"Yeah. It sort of looked like it, didn't it?" Pa shook his head. "But somehow I don't feel like jumping around and yelling about it. For ten years I been trying to get even with him, and now I done it, busting him down like that before all his men. But I ain't too happy about it."

"Maybe we ought to have let him hang you," Boston said. "If we'd known it was going to make you so darned unhappy—"

"Never figured on getting hung," Pa said. "Not with you and Cissie around. Of course, the rest of you helped some."

Harve flashed his gold tooth. "That's real nice of you to say so, Pa."

"I was scared to death," Casey said, "until I began to understand you had a plan worked out."

The Braggs looked at each other. "Plan?" Eldon said. "The only plan we had was to stay alive, somehow."

"We didn't even know if Boston could get out of that tunnel back there, what with all the snow," Pinky said, "or even what he was going to do if he did get out."

Boston grinned. "We were all in the same boat. I didn't know, either."

"To tell the truth, I thought you'd gone to sleep back there," Pa said.

"I did," Boston said, "But that big act you put on, moaning and yelling, woke me up, so I tromped across the roof to see what the fuss was all about."

The whole bunch of them should have been on the stage, Casey thought.

She began to warm up the food that had gone cold on the table.

# CHAPTER 15

*"This office has the same number of men as it did in 1886, when Doc Shores was sheriff, but crime is a little more complex today. Doc loved to spend most of his time trailing horse thieves, with about two days a month in the office. We've still got the horse thieves and rustlers. They spring up like weeds back in those hills. It's tough today to get convictions, or to make them stick after you do get them. The last rustler I took to the pen beat me home with a pardon from the Governor in his hand."* George Cope, Sheriff, Gunnison County, Colorado; Gunnison, 1965.


THE STORM THAT MADE THE LONG RIDE HOME miserable for Ross Chamberlain's men was the forerunner of many that struck with varying intensity during the following six weeks. The Braggs stuck close to home, except for two trips to Gunnison, during one of which Harve slept part of the night on a bench in the county courtroom while the city marshal looked diligently for him all over town to throw him in jail for a disturbance at a house on the West Side where a husband had come home unexpectedly.

In early April a great chinook wind came sweeping across the mountains, blowing its warm breath on the snowfields, settling them and glazing them faintly yellow. An area of brown stubble began to show around the lonesome Army mower in the meadow, and the snow receded away from the buildings. Casey heard water from the geese pond gurgling under the lumpy ice below the dam.

For some time she had been watching the greening of grass that grew in a line directly under the drip edge of the house roof. She was kneeling there one warm afternoon, looking at the brown litter of dead grass that protected the fresh new blades, when Pa stopped behind her and said, "You're about ready to leave us, ain't you, Cissie?"

She looked at him quickly.

"Sure now. I've seen it coming for a couple of weeks."

He was so totally unlike her father that she wondered why she had come to regard him as a father. But it was true.

They went inside. Casey carried the teapot to the kettle. "I never figured I'd ever drink a cup of that slop," Pa said, "but I kind of like it now." He paused "When?"

"Tomorrow?"

"All right. When you make up your mind, that's the thing to do, Cissie—make the move."

She poured his tea. He liked it weak, more for the warmth than the taste. Pa always held a cup in the palm of his hand, seldom using the handle. That was only one of the little things she had come to notice about him.

"I know the others pestered you to marry them," Pa said. "Did Boston ever get around to it?"

"Yes, he did."

"Boston's a good man, Cissie. You wouldn't have gone wrong there."

"I thought the same way, Pa, but I couldn't do it. It wouldn't have been right."

"Uh-huh." Pa slupped his tea. "No-good husband somewhere?"

Again his shrewdness made Casey eye him sharply.

"Yes, I do have a husband, but he isn't a no-good. I was the worthless one in that bargain."

"Are you figuring to go back to him?"

"Oh, no. That's all over and done."

Pa nodded. "Not back to your folks, either?"

"No. I'm going someplace where no one knows me, and I won't make the mistake I made at Cimarron of looking the way I did."

"Well, now, maybe it wasn't a mistake," Pa said slowly. "I didn't see you then, but I've sure heard plenty of talk about how you looked and acted. Maybe it was a good thing, because it made you fight every minute of the day to change folks' minds, mainly right here, but that's where it counted because that's where you was."

They were silent for a while.

"Tomorrow," Pa said. "Kids like you don't know how fast tomorrow comes to somebody my age. It's been pretty good to have you around here, Cissie. I've come to think high of you, and so have the boys."

Pa compressed his lips tight. He got up suddenly, and then Casey found herself clinging to him and crying. He patted her on the back gently. "Doggone short-haired whelp. Stop that blubbering."

"I feel like blubbering."

"Write us a letter sometime." After a while Pa set her aside and went to his room. When he returned, he took her hand in his big paw and dumped ten gold coins into it. "There's a hundred bucks, Cissie, and don't spend it all in one place. It just happens to be honest money, too."

"But you don't owe me that much, Pa."

"Don't tell me what I owe you! There you go, running the whole ranch again."

"But Pinky already gave me—"

"I ain't responsible for what he did. That boy does

215

nothing but get me in trouble. That's what I owe you, and I don't want no argument." Pa walked out of the house. Casey heard him yell at the dogs, "Go chase something, you worthless varmints!"

That night at supper Casey thought back to the first meal she had served at the same table, remembering how tired and scared she had been, and the appalling speed with which the Braggs had devoured everything in sight. They tasted their food now and ate more slowly, an improvement which she had brought about gradually.

She recalled, too, how it had seemed to her that Pa had been taken in with the jug that Christmas Eve, leaving her to the mercies of his sons, but she knew now that he had been putting her to a severe test and that afterward he had been on her side all the way. She would be forever grateful for the amazing understanding of that rough-cut, blustery old man.

Once more she felt like blubbering.

"How come it's so awful quiet around here tonight?" Eldon asked.

"Because Cissie has finally learned you not to eat like hogs," Pa said. "Now you got time to hear if something's being said or not. Pass the gravy, Harve."

Casey saw Boston watching her with a thoughtful expression. He knew she was leaving, she thought. Perhaps Pa had told him, but it was more likely that he had sensed it for himself; he was like his father when it came to seeing and understanding things that his brothers missed.

After supper Boston stalled around until he was alone with Pa and Casey. "You're leaving us, huh?"

Casey nodded. "Tomorrow. I'll go to Sapinero and catch the afternoon train."

"To where?" Boston asked.

Casey shook her head.

Pa got up from the table. "I think I'll go see about—"

"No need, Pa." Boston smiled. "I asked her once to marry me. When she said no, I knew she meant it." He paused a moment at the door. "Good luck, Casey."

It was the last she ever saw of Boston. Before dawn the next morning he was gone, leaving a note to his brothers saying that he had ridden to Old Camp.

Pa broke the news of Casey's leaving at breakfast. His sons argued loudly against it, and Eldon, never subtle, renewed his proposal of marriage right there. Then Pinky and Harve felt they had no choice but to make their bids also. Casey shook her head at all of them, and then she had to go to her room for a few minutes to regain her composure.

When she returned, Eldon said, "Anyway, we'll all go down with you, and if anybody as much as stares out of the corner of his eye, I'll bust him in two!"

"No," Pa said, "we ain't going. I don't want nobody to associate Cissie with us when she gets on that train. She can take the buckskin and leave him at the livery barn."

"She can't carry her looking glass," Pinky said. "I'll have to go with her. Won't I, Casey?"

"I'm leaving the mirror for your sisters." No longer did the mirror have any hold on Casey. The day before she had started to take a long look at herself in it, but she did not have to do it; what she knew about herself was inside her and could not have been reflected from a glass surface.

"You didn't give her much help getting here, Pinky," Pa said. "I think she can follow a plain road getting out to Sap, and from there— Well, I reckon Cissie can go anywhere she wants to now in good style."

"I hope you're right, Pa," Casey said.

"I'm always right!" Pa blustered. "Pinky, get down to the barn and ride the winter kinks out of that buckskin."

Casey put the house in order for the last time, and then she took a short walk around the ranch. She fed the geese. She looked at Mrs. Bragg's garden plot, just emerging from the snow. For a few minutes she stood in the hayloft.

The dogs padded along beside her when she started back to the house. She looked once in the direction of Old Camp. In every woman's life, she thought, there must be one face that would never fade from sharp remembrance.

She looked around the kitchen. It seemed to her that it had always been the way it was now. She made no effort to recall the way it had looked when she first walked into it. The clothes that Ma Jensen had lent her, along with Riley's gloves, were neatly folded on her bed. Pa had promised to return them the first time he went to Cimarron. Her carpetbag was packed, with even less than she had brought, for she had worn out one dress and had only the plain, mended one that she was wearing.

The taffeta dress Pinky had given her was under the extra quilts in the trunk. The Bragg girls would discover it one day, and quite likely it would fit one of them.

She looked into the storeroom. Before long the Braggs were going to need more supplies. Pa's room was next. For a moment Casey considered lighting a lamp to look into the narrow passage between it and the pantry, but that had not been part of her daily routine, and so she turned away.

The flintlock rifle caught her attention next. Just standing there looking at it, she realized why she had made the final tour: When she left home she had not said good-bye to anyone or to anything, but now she was starting again, wiser, with the determination not to run at life with headlong disregard of herself and others.

Pa stopped in the doorway. "Take that worthless rifle along with you. You got so you could shoot it like an old Indian fighter. Take the darned thing."

Casey saw herself getting on the train with her worn carpetbag and a long rifle. "No, Pa, it belongs here. Someday I'll come back and shoot it again."

Pa shook his head. "You'll never come back." He came across the room and kissed her gently on the forehead. "So long, little short hair."

They brought the buckskin to the door. Pinky tried to look tough and unconcerned. Nothing had changed about Eldon; he was still a huge, ugly man, but he no longer looked like an ape, a brute, to Casey. And Harve—he never would change; you had to take him for what he was.

Casey kissed them one by one. Harve let his hands stray. She punched him in the solar plexus with two doubled fingers, catching him so sharply that he gasped. "Ow!" he said, and grinned.

Eldon boosted her into the uncomfortable side saddle, which she did not intend to use like a lady as soon as she was out of sight. She settled herself and looked down at Pa. "I forgot to ask. Did you ever make up your mind about letting me stay?"

"Still thinking on it, Cissie, still thinking on it."

The dogs followed her until she told them to go back. They sat down then and watched her. A hundred yards away, she looked back. The Braggs were standing where she had left them. She raised her hand when they waved.

Then she heard Pa's booming shout for the last time, "Get around!"

Her eyes wet with tears, Casey rode on.

We hope that you enjoyed reading this
Sagebrush Large Print Western.
If you would like to read more Sagebrush titles,
ask your librarian or contact the Publishers:

## United States and Canada

Thomas T. Beeler, *Publisher*
Post Office Box 659
Hampton Falls, New Hampshire 03844-0659
(800) 818-7574

## United Kingdom, Eire, and the Republic of South Africa

Isis Publishing Ltd.
7 Centremead
Osney Mead
Oxford OX2 0ES  England
(01865) 250333

## Australia and New Zealand

Bolinda Publishing Pty. Ltd.
17 Mohr Street
Tullamarine, 3043, Victoria, Australia
(016103) 9338 0666